A CHRISTMAS AT HOTEL DEL CORONADO

ROMANCE AT THE GILDED AGE RESORTS
BOOK NINE

KATHLEEN DENLY

Cheryl,
It's a pleasure having you on my launch team again.
You are a treasure!
Kathleen Denly

WILD HEART
BOOKS

To James Asher, my ninth grade high school English teacher, for encouraging (and never laughing at) my fledgling attempts at writing and helping me to believe in my gift.

"Prove all things; hold fast that which is good."

— 1 THESSALONIANS 5:21 KJV

CHAPTER 1

Thursday, November 24, 1892
Hotel del Coronado, Coronado, California

*E*leanore Wainright should have escaped with
her aunt when she'd had the chance.

Now she stood trapped by etiquette at the edge of
the circular drive of the magnificent Hotel del Coronado. She struggled to keep her polite smile in place as
her father and James Mitchell—the heir her father had
brought her here to claim as a husband—prattled on
about the latest developments in the production of
steel. The two men were oblivious to the elegant
wooden hotel's sandcastle-like architecture, the
rhythmic crash of waves against the nearby beach, and
the occasional cry of seagulls.

Her lips grew dry as a cold gust of wind threatened
to tug her hat free and played with a loose strand of her

blond hair. She shoved her hat pin deeper and tucked the wayward lock behind her ear. Neither man appeared aware of her discomfort. Would they even notice if she let herself frown or yawn, revealing her utter boredom with the conversation? Not likely. Still, she dared not risk it.

If only she'd followed wise Aunt Gladys's example and declared a headache the moment the two men crossed paths and escaped to their suite thirty minutes ago. If she had, Eleanore could be writing the next scene in her latest mystery novel that called to her as one of Homer's Sirens called to the sailors in his *Odyssey*. Much like those alluring monsters would end the lives of unsuspecting men, her career as a mystery author, if ever discovered, would end Father's dreams of seeing her well matched. Thus, she was forced to write in secret. Now would be the perfect time to put down a few more words, but duty kept her in place while the two men continued speaking as though she were not present.

The approaching chuff and clatter of the island's steam train and passenger car drew her attention as the transport came to a stop several yards from the hotel. A handful of people disembarked, but it was a woman dressed in an elegant black silk dress beneath an out-of-fashion sealskin sacque coat who sparked Eleanore's curiosity. A large black hat bearing a thin black veil shrouded her visage.

The woman carried her own valise, and though she

repeatedly checked over her shoulder as she proceeded toward the resort, no one seemed to pay her any mind. Was she traveling alone? She appeared rather young to be a widow. Eleanore would guess her to be no older than her own twenty years. And Eleanore was an excellent judge of age, having devoted years to studying those around her.

She examined the remaining guests who'd separated themselves from the other passengers by directing their steps toward the hotel. They'd divided into small groups.

At the front of the nearing group, a young couple was trailed by a female servant tending two small children. Several feet behind them, a middle-aged couple strolled ahead of two servants, no doubt their valet and lady's maid. Another couple in less fine clothes walked a few feet behind them. Just in front of the odd woman in black, an older gentleman strode alone, tapping a cane that was clearly unnecessary.

For a moment, Eleanore considered that perhaps he was the woman's escort, but the two exchanged no glances, and the gentleman continued on with no apparent thought for the woman trailing farther and farther behind him.

Her steps were slow, almost awkward, as if each movement pained her. As she drew close, her complexion revealed itself to be unusually pale. Eleanore bit the inside of her lip. Was the woman ill?

Eleanore scanned the scene again. Perhaps she'd

missed someone who might be accompanying the woman. But no. Only hotel staff, busy transferring trunks and other luggage from the train to a wagon, remained near the station.

James and her father continued their conversation without a glance at the newly arrived guests who passed by and strode up the grand stairs leading to the hotel's wide, wraparound porch and main entrance.

All but the woman in black.

In confirmation of Eleanore's conclusion, the woman slowly made her way toward the stairs which led to the entry for unaccompanied women. Although designed to disguise such guest's lack of protection until they could blend in with married and accompanied single guests within the resort, the effectiveness of the separate entrance was rather doubtful, given its location mere feet past the main doors.

The beautiful stranger set her gloved hand on the rail and hesitated before the first step, as if gathering her strength to ascend the eleven stairs to the covered veranda.

Eleanore opened her mouth, preparing to interrupt Father's conversation with a request that he assist the woman, but before she could utter a word, one of the hotel's bellboys dashed down the steps. The brown-haired man took the woman's valise and offered her his arm.

"Allow me to assist you, ma'am." He glanced

around, clearly searching for her escort, but his walnut-brown eyes snagged on Eleanore and widened.

Eleanore's breath stopped, all sound vanished, and the world itself faded away as she gazed at the face she'd expected to never see again. It couldn't be Thomas. But it was. Despite his unfamiliar uniform, there was no chance she'd mistake the sight of her childhood friend who'd grown into the man who stole her heart, promised to love her always, then disappeared the next day.

He gaped at her, a storm of emotions flashing in his eyes. Then he blinked, and the tempest was replaced with a formal indifference. He turned from her to address the woman in black. "Is your escort retrieving the rest of your belongings?"

In words so quiet Eleanore strained to hear her, the woman replied, "I'm afraid my brother—a physician—was unexpectedly detained in Orange. He mistakenly kept my claim tickets, and that callous San Diego station master refused to release my luggage."

"I'm sorry to hear that. I'll ask my supervisor if there's anything that can be done to help you." Thomas slowly assisted her up the stairs.

Her voice grew stronger. "Thank you, but my brother will arrive soon. The best help would be to make certain the front desk clerks know to inform me the moment my brother arrives. His name is Malcolm Berdan. It is vital there be no delay in informing me. He has done so much for me, I must ready myself and greet him promptly."

Thomas opened the door. "Yes, ma'am. I'll see to informing the clerks."

The woman paused before entering. "I want your word that you will do this."

"You have it."

Eleanore couldn't restrain her snort as the woman nodded and entered the hotel. As if Thomas Harding's word was worth anything.

The sound must have been loud because Thomas's confused gaze shot to hers. For a moment, he seemed to search her expression. Then, with a frown, he followed the strange woman inside.

"Is something wrong, dear?" Father's voice drew her attention from the closing door. His words and tone expressed concern, but his slate-blue eyes held irritation.

Eleanore's face warmed as she glanced at James. Though she'd met him just three days prior, she'd studied him enough to confidently judge his emotions. Rather than furrowed, his brow was slightly raised, and his mocha-brown eyes were open. So he wasn't annoyed by her rude interruption, merely curious. Thank goodness.

Father had made it abundantly clear that, while he had pressing business matters to attend during their winter's stay at the beautiful new seaside resort and hunting lodge, her sole purpose was to win James

Mitchell's affection and secure a proposal from him that would gain her membership among New York's most elite society.

Although Father had earned millions through his various steel and railroad businesses, he'd been born the son of a humble factory owner—a sin New York's high society refused to forgive. In contrast, the Mitchells' old money meant automatic inclusion, even among McCallister's list of the four hundred families invited to Caroline Astor's ballroom each year. Such an invitation would not only open every door in New York for Eleanore and Father, it would mean access to new business opportunities Father couldn't otherwise attain.

With Father scrutinizing her, Eleanore drew a breath and lowered her chin. "No, nothing is wrong, Father. Something tickled my nose, but it's gone. Please excuse my interruption."

The men resumed their conversation, and Eleanore did her best to remain still and quiet while her mind whirled.

What was Thomas doing in Coronado, California? After his shocking disappearance two years ago, Father had explained that Thomas had accepted an arranged marriage to a sickly young heiress in San Francisco in exchange for a prestigious position managing a bank. The arrangement was quite a step up for the son of their housekeeper, and Father, unaware of Thomas's promises to Eleanore, was rightfully proud of facilitating the engagement. Was it possible Thomas's young bride had already passed away? Yet, if she had, he'd be far too wealthy to require the income of a mere bellboy. So what was he doing here?

She studied Father. He didn't appear to have noticed Thomas. What would he think of the coincidence? No doubt he'd be displeased and would remind her what an unsuitable and unacceptable match Thomas would make. Not that she needed any reminder. Thomas may have been a devoted friend when they were children, but the boy she thought she'd known and loved had grown into a man whose choices she didn't recognize and couldn't respect.

Her gaze drifted back to the door. If he worked here, was there any chance she could avoid seeing him again during the four months her father had planned for them to stay? It was what a sensible woman would wish for. Yet the mystery of his presence here tugged as strongly as her unfinished novel.

～

*T*hough his heart hammered against his ribs, Thomas maintained a polite expression as he escorted Miss Lottie Berdan to the stairs nearest her assigned room. What was Eleanore doing here? Of all the luxurious resorts in the country, why had she and her father, Rupert Wainright, come to one on the opposite side of the continent?

Mother would've called it providence, but Thomas

struggled to see God's loving hand in bringing the woman who'd broken his heart back into his life.

"How much farther?" Miss Berdan's soft, plaintive voice interrupted his thoughts.

Thomas blinked at their surroundings and realized he'd passed the staircase. Cheeks warm, he pivoted to face the weary woman trailing him. "My sincerest apologies. I'm afraid my thoughts wandered." He gestured behind her. "If you'll return to the stairs we recently passed, I'll take you up to your room."

Miss Berdan heaved a sigh before following his instructions. At least she didn't scold him. Was she too frail to speak the words? He pressed his lips together, determined to remain focused on getting the poor guest to her room without further delay. It was clear from her black garb that she was in mourning.

With Miss Berdan's painfully slow gait, it took far longer than usual to reach the less expensive third floor. Mindful of his pace, he led the way to her room and opened the door for her. Once she'd stepped inside, he pointed out the amenities, including the shared bath down the hall. Then he handed her the key and asked whether she needed anything else.

"Yes. I understand there is a drugstore on the premises. Where can I find it?"

"It's on the ground floor near the rotunda."

"Rotunda?"

"That's what we call our lobby. Would you like me to show you?"

"Thank you, no. I think I'll rest first."

After she assured him she needed no further assistance, he stepped outside and shut the door.

He stared at the white-painted surface, seeing instead two large, ornately carved and darkly stained doors with polished golden handles. Two years ago, rain had dripped down his face as he stood, debating whether to bang his fist on the entry to the Wainrights' New York mansion and demand to speak to Eleanore in person rather than wait for her reply to the farewell message her coldhearted father had begrudgingly allowed him to write her.

If Thomas hadn't himself slipped the missive beneath her bedroom door as she slept, he'd wonder whether she'd received the letter. Her lack of response was so unlike her...except that she'd always worshipped the ground her father walked on. Thomas had been a fool to believe she'd choose him over her only remaining parent and the life of luxury she'd been born to. Despite her vows the day before he'd spoken to her father, her silence soon made it clear that time, consideration, and love for her father had overruled the love she'd professed for Thomas.

Some might accuse Thomas of choosing money over love, but he knew the truth. He'd foolishly believed that explaining his reasons for accepting Rupert's money and the terms that came with it would convince Eleanore to forgive him and wait for his return. But it seemed Rupert had known her better.

Thomas finally turned from Miss Berdan's door. He traipsed back downstairs and made his way toward the front of the hotel.

Please, Lord, let Eleanore be gone. Let her have been visiting a guest with her father while staying elsewhere in the area. Don't let them be registered here.

What would he do if they were guests here and he was summoned to their suite? Thomas wasn't ready to see her again—didn't know how he would ever be ready to see her.

CHAPTER 2

 he thought of encountering Thomas again had kept Eleanore on edge since seeing him. Yesterday, she'd feigned a headache to hide away in her room and write, avoiding any potential encounter with him. But today they were leaving the island resort and Thomas behind. At least until sunset.

Following Aunt Gladys, Eleanore preceded her father onto the ferry that would take them across the bay to San Diego. Minutes later, the odd little boat began its journey, and Eleanore drew a deep breath then released it.

Father had arranged for them to join James on an expedition to the sea caves in La Jolla, a small coastal town north of San Diego. Eleanore had heard much about the rugged cliffs and hidden wonders found within the caverns which were only accessible by canoe. As she was not a strong swimmer, the notion of braving the ocean waves in such a small vessel made her nervous, but the stories she'd been told created an eagerness to explore that overruled her fear.

The ferry ride across the bay took only minutes, and soon they were making their way along the bustling streets of San Diego.

James stood outside the livery where he'd said to meet him, but his back was to them. A woman in a familiar black dress, sacque coat, and veiled black hat stood near him. They did not face each other, but were their mouths moving in conversation? Before she could be certain, James spun and waved at Eleanore and Father with a smile. In the same instant, the woman strode away. Neither person spared the other a glance. Eleanore must have imagined their conversation. The woman had merely paused for traffic before crossing the road.

The brim of her black hat bent up with a strong gust, revealing a glimpse of the woman's profile before lowering again. Miss Berdan? What was the ill woman doing so far from the hotel? As weary as she'd appeared on her arrival, she had surely come to the resort for health reasons. Eleanore had predicted the woman would spend her time taking in the medicinal sea air from the hotel's veranda, if not entirely in her room. Yet there was no question the odd woman had just scurried across the street with impressive speed and disappeared around the corner of the nearest building.

Eleanore scrunched her lips to one side, eyes

narrowed. Rarely was she so mistaken in her assessment of a person. In fact, the only time she'd been *this* wrong had been in her estimation of Thomas. Her stomach knotted at the reminder. What was he doing today? She had no notion of a hotel employee's usual schedule. Would he be working, or might he have the day off? She scanned the streets but saw no other familiar figures.

"Miss Wainright, such a pleasure." Mercifully, James's greeting of her aunt interrupted Eleanore's shifting thoughts.

Aunt Gladys dipped her chin. "As it is to see you, Mr. Mitchell. Though I admit, I still have my doubts about this plan of yours."

He laughed. "Where's your sense of adventure?"

"I'm afraid I left it in my youth along with a naive belief in my own invincibility."

He placed his hand over his heart. "I assure you, no harm shall befall you in my presence."

Aunt Gladys harumphed, but her lips were curled at the corners, and her cornflower-blue eyes sparkled with amusement.

James seized Eleanore's fingers. "Eleanore, my dear, how glad I am you could join us." He lifted her hand to kiss the air above her knuckles. "I rather missed you yesterday. I do hope your headache is gone."

"It is. Thank you for asking. Was that Miss Berdan I saw a moment ago?" She glanced past him, but the lady in black was gone.

He released her with a frown and replied without looking about. "I have no idea whom you are referring to." He faced her father. "Rupert, I am so glad you could all make it. I have heard marvelous things about these caves, and I'm certain the adventure will be all the more delightful in your presence."

Eleanore forced a smile as Father made his polite reply. It had not escaped her notice that James was equally effusive with each person he met, so long as he deemed them someone of consequence. For Father's sake, she tried to overlook the unctuous, though benign, behavior.

James made a slight bow and swung his arm toward the livery as though presenting the crown jewels. "As promised, I have hired their best carriage to transport us to La Jolla where our canoes await. I have also packed us a delicious picnic lunch which we will enjoy upon our arrival and before setting out to sea. So"—he offered Eleanore his arm—"shall we proceed?"

She laid her hand on his arm, and he patted it as he led her inside. "I am quite eager for you to experience the breathtaking beauty of the sea caves." He lowered his voice and leaned close to her ear. "I've heard they can be rather romantic."

Uncertain how to respond, Eleanore glanced at Father, who merely beamed at her. Clearly, he approved of James's intimate behavior. If only she could feel an ounce of the pleasure radiating from Father's eyes.

~

*L*ater that evening, Eleanore gazed through the large glass windows enclosing the abundantly wide porch of the Hotel del Coronado as she took a sip of her hot chocolate. She pressed her foot onto the wood slats of the veranda, setting her rocking chair in motion as a cool ocean breeze blew in through the open doors.

To Eleanore's right, Father and James now debated whether the dozen rabbits caught that morning by James's friend, Anthony, was a greater coup than the two-hundred-forty-pound sea bass Father's friend had caught off the hotel's pier. Neither man seemed the least bit fatigued by their boating excursion. Probably because the men they'd hired to guide them to the caves had done all the paddling.

Despite a beautiful, clear sky, the canoe she'd shared with James had rocked violently over wave after wave. The delicious seafood and fruit picnic James had provided had churned in her stomach. James had prattled on about the discovery of the caves, but Eleanore couldn't bring herself to concentrate on his words.

The afternoon spent in the sun had drained most of her energy. Nevertheless, visiting the caves and being splashed by a pair of passing seals had been a fun adventure she wouldn't soon forget.

On her left, Aunt Gladys, resplendent in her dinner attire, set her empty cup and saucer on a small side table. A moment later, her eyes drifted closed. Moonlight glinted off the woman's silver hair, reminding Eleanore of the nearly two decades that separated Father from his elder sister. No doubt, Aunt Gladys would soon wish to retire for the evening—the excuse Eleanore was waiting for.

Last night, fatigue and drooping eyelids had forced her to leave the heroine of her latest novel in the middle of picking the lock to her employer's office. Over dinner, inspiration had struck regarding how the heroine would find the evidence she was searching for. Eleanore had made a note on the small notepad she kept in her pocket but was eager to see how the idea played out.

Eleanore opened her mouth to suggest she and Aunt Gladys retire to their rooms, but the sight of a figure striding onto the veranda stilled her tongue. *Thomas.* Without thought, her gaze found his hands. No ring. Thomas had once told her that, although many men chose not to, he wanted to wear a ring when he was married as a reminder of the gift God had blessed him with. Did his lack of adornment now mean he was widowed...or had never married? Her heart stuttered. Was there a chance he'd reconsidered and not gone through with his plans? If so, why hadn't he contacted her? She forced a deep breath despite her tightening airway. More probably, he'd merely changed his mind. After all, he'd changed his mind about marrying *her*.

Thomas approached a young woman farther down the veranda and said something Eleanore couldn't hear.

A soft laugh escaped the woman's lips as she placed her hand on Thomas's arm.

Eleanore's teeth clenched. She was such a fool. She slammed her cup onto the wooden arm of her rocking chair. Hot liquid splattered everything in a two-foot radius.

Aunt Gladys's eyes flew open. "My goodness. What happened?"

"Oh dear." Eleanore drew her handkerchief from her sleeve and began dabbing at the brown liquid puddling on her purple skirt and speckling her bodice and sleeves. Her handkerchief quickly saturated, rendering itself useless.

Footsteps rushed over. "Here, let me help."

Eleanore looked up to find Thomas offering her a napkin.

Before she could speak, Father stepped between them and yanked the cloth from Thomas's grasp. "Thank you. You may go."

Thomas's frustrated gaze met hers. "But...I want to he—"

"Your assistance is unnecessary," Father insisted. "Now go. Be about your duties."

Why was Father being so rude? Even if he recognized Thomas, Father had no idea of the heartbreak Thomas had caused her.

"Here." James drew her attention with his proffered handkerchief.

She reached for the cloth, and tiny brown droplets

flung themselves from the drenched cuff of her sleeve to James's pristine white shirt, vest, and tailcoat.

She gasped. "I'm so sorry."

"Don't worry about it. Accidents happen," James reassured her as Father offered James his handkerchief.

James used Father's handkerchief to remove the spots from his clothes. Then he collected the soiled handkerchiefs and offered to have them washed and returned.

Eleanore stood. "No, please. I'm the one who made the mess. I should be the one to see to these." She reached for the cloths, but James pulled them out of her reach and caught her hand with his free one.

"Caring for you is my privilege." He lifted her sticky fingers and kissed her knuckles, his dark brown gaze never straying from hers. "You wouldn't deny me this pleasure, would you?"

Confusion swirled within her. She searched for Thomas, to see what he thought of James's open affection, but he was gone—slipping away in the night, as silently as he'd left her two years ago.

～

Two days later, Eleanore paused on a bustling street in San Diego and tipped her face toward the sun, her eyes closed. She soaked in the warmth that seemed so at odds with the early Christmas season. Back in New York, she and her aunt would be bundled in layers and rushing from store to store in an effort to spend as little time as possible in the frigid wind and sometimes snow. Here, patrons strolled comfortably along the sidewalks in clothing better suited for a warm New York autumn.

When she opened her eyes, they caught on the window display of a milliner's shop. A tiny potted pine tree decorated with a string of popcorn stood beside a beautiful lavender picture hat. The headpiece was exactly the type her mother would have purchased. Purple had been Mother's favorite color, and she'd have adored the large silk flowers and white feathers tucked into the dark-purple ribbon.

Aunt Gladys had continued walking before seeming to notice that Eleanore was no longer at her side. She turned back to join Eleanore at the window. "It's a lovely hat. Should we go inside?"

Eleanore shook her head. "I only stopped because it reminded me of Mother."

Aunt Gladys hummed. "Yes, it is rather more ornate than your usual simpler tastes. I do think your mother would have loved it."

Not that she'd have worn it. Eleanore's few memories of her mother involved buoyant, day-long shopping trips contrasted by weeks of knocking on the locked door to her mother's darkened bedroom.

Aunt Gladys checked the timepiece pinned to her bodice. "Rupert's meeting won't end for at least another two hours. Where should we go next?"

Eleanore mentally ticked off each of the Christmas gifts she'd already purchased as she considered the shops lining the street ahead. Many of the storefronts bore Christmas decorations to catch the eye of passing shoppers. One even had its display glass painted in wintery scenes that seemed out of place in sunny California. She settled on a general store whose window display of assorted children's toys was topped by a plain wreath bearing a red bow. "We haven't been in there yet."

"I'm not sure we'll find anything worth purchasing, but why not?"

They stepped inside the store and discovered a wide variety of goods from scented soaps to sledgehammers. Candies, premade dresses, children's toys, and even large farming tools filled the shelves lining the walls. Aunt Gladys wandered toward a display of Christmas cards. But it was the racks of rifles and pistols hanging on the far back wall that caught Eleanore's attention. Or more precisely, the woman standing in front of them.

Once again, Miss Berdan was not where she ought to be. Eleanore gaped as the store owner demonstrated for the pale-faced woman how to load and shoot a pistol.

Another man's voice spoke so close, Eleanore nearly jumped out of her skin. "That there ain't no gift, no matter what she says."

Eleanore turned to ask his meaning, but it was clear the man hadn't been speaking to her. He was seated on one side of a barrel topped with a checkerboard and was addressing his competitor. Both men seem to have forgotten their game and fixed their eyes on Miss Berdan.

The other man replied, "You ain't wrong. I got a nickel that says she's gonna do herself harm with that there weapon."

The first man shook his head. "No bet. Look at her, she's suffering something awful and that's for certain."

"Shame too. She's a right purty one."

Eleanore's heart constricted. Could the men be right?

Across the shop, Miss Berdan's hands trembled as she practiced loading the weapon. Her actions were so shaky that the store owner snatched the pistol back and quickly removed the bullets. He told her the amount for the gun and the bullets. She gave him money, and he wrapped her purchases in paper before handing them over.

Miss Berdan shuffled toward the exit, her eyes on the ground. She came within two feet of Eleanore before noticing her. "Oh dear." The woman's black-gloved hand fluttered at her throat as she stepped back. "My apologies. I ought to have been paying more attention to where I was going."

Eleanore offered a warm smile. "No apology needed. I should have stepped aside, but I was hoping for a moment to speak with you."

Miss Berdan's expression grew wary.

Eleanore floundered. What could she say? She desperately wanted to deny the suspicions of the gossiping men, but it wasn't the first time she'd overheard similar predictions about a suffering soul. She couldn't bear to stand by while another person made such a desperate choice. If there was any truth to the men's speculation, Eleanore must find a way to convince Miss Berdan that all hope was not lost.

Aunt Gladys joined them with a smile she directed at Miss Berdan. "Hello. I am Gladys Wainright, and this is my niece, Miss Eleanore Wainright."

Miss Berdan dipped her chin. "Pleased to meet you. I'm Miss Lottie Berdan."

Aunt Gladys eyed Lottie from head to toe with pursed lips. "Haven't I seen you at the hotel?" Her aunt spoke as if there were only one hotel nearby, when in truth there were several. Though her father would argue the Hotel del Coronado was the only establishment worth noting.

Miss Berdan seemed to understand and nodded.

Aunt Gladys jerked her head in satisfaction. "I thought so. I was about to suggest to my niece that we take a break from our shopping endeavors and enjoy a meal. Would you care to join us?"

Bless Aunt Gladys. This was the perfect solution. Dining together would give Eleanore the opportunity to have a seemingly casual conversation in which she could ferret out whether or not Miss Berdan intended to harm herself.

Lottie's gaze flashed with surprise, her gloved hands quivering slightly. "I...I would be honored," she replied softly, a hint of gratitude in her voice.

As they left the shop, Eleanore silently begged God for discernment and the right words to reach Miss Berdan. Regardless of the answers their conversation produced, Eleanore was determined to offer Lottie the companionship and support she seemed to desperately need. Whatever Father's plans for their stay were, perhaps God had brought Eleanore to California to bring a glimmer of light into the mysterious woman's shadowed world.

CHAPTER 3

*E*leanore sat with her aunt and Lottie at a table near the center of the grand restaurant. The soft glow of gas lamps illuminated the establishment's intricately patterned wallpaper and rich mahogany tables with matching high-back chairs upholstered in plush velvet. Draped in evergreen garland, a chandelier hung from the ceiling, its sparkling crystals catching the light and casting shimmering patterns across the room. Hints of pine mingled with the tantalizing aroma of the cuisine being served. Small potted poinsettias adorned each table. The gentle murmur of conversation was punctuated by the occasional clink of silverware against fine china.

Lottie smiled as their waiter hurried away to inform the kitchen of their arrival. "It is so kind of you to invite me. I'm afraid I've been rather lonely since my arrival."

"Nonsense, it's our pleasure," Eleanore assured her.

"Thank you for agreeing to join us. We spend so much time in each other's company that we sometimes run out of topics to discuss. It is refreshing to have you with us."

Aunt Gladys's nose wrinkled. "I admit, I haven't quite adjusted to this strange new idea of an unmarried woman being permitted to travel unaccompanied. It simply wasn't done in my day."

"This wasn't my choice, I assure you." Lottie's tremulous fingers traced from her temple to her chin before disappearing beneath the table. "My brother had promised to escort me. And he did accompany me from Detroit to Orange. But as the train was about to depart from Orange, he received word that a woman had fainted at the station. Despite my pointing out that there must be another doctor in that town who could assist her, my brother disembarked at the last possible moment, leaving me no choice but to continue on alone."

Understanding dawned in Aunt Gladys's cornflower eyes, and her expression softened. "How trying that must have been for you, dear."

The notion of traveling unescorted seemed exhilarating to Eleanore, but she didn't expect she would feel the same if she were ailing as Lottie appeared to be.

Lottie's shoulders slumped. "Indeed, it was. Particularly because it wasn't until I reached San Diego that I realized my brother still had the claim tickets for our luggage."

Aunt Gladys placed a hand upon her chest. "Oh my. To be without your belongings in a strange city must be quite distressing."

Lottie nodded, a wistful smile ghosting across her lips. "But I am grateful for the opportunity to make new acquaintances. If my brother were with me, you might not have taken pity on me and invited me to dine with you."

Eleanore wrung her fingers in her lap. She yearned to aid the unfortunate woman, but social convention would protest the only means she could think of. Oh, dash it all. Surely, God would want her to help, and that trumped any of society's rules. "Please do not think me impertinent, but I believe you and I are similar in size. I'm afraid I do not have anything in black, but I did bring a lovely gray ensemble. I would be pleased to loan it to you until your brother arrives."

Aunt Gladys's head jerked back. "Eleanore, dear, what are you thinking? You'll embarrass our guest."

"Not at all." Lottie glanced toward her left as though checking whether others were listening, but her smile brightened. "You are a truly generous soul, but I'm afraid it is more than clothing I lack, or I would not hazard these trips to San Diego. You see, my medication is also in my luggage."

"Have you informed the stationmaster of this?" Aunt Gladys asked.

"Yes, but I'm afraid it made no difference." Lottie's arms moved as though she were wringing her hands in

27

her lap. "Without my claim tickets, he will not permit me to retrieve my luggage."

Guilt slammed into Eleanore. She ought to have spoken with Lottie sooner. To think of the young woman suffering all this time broke Eleanore's heart. "Please tell me the name of this medication, and I will ensure the hotel's pharmacist has it delivered to your room as soon as we return."

Lottie's expression tightened. Had Eleanore overstepped? "I appreciate your generosity, Eleanore," she murmured. "But I have had this ailment since childhood, and my brother is the only one who knows how to make the medicine."

Eleanore bit the inside of her cheek, recalling the reason for her concerns and inviting Lottie to dine with them. Was it possible Lottie had been this ill her entire life, or was her illness getting worse? Either might explain tragic thoughts.

Lord, give me the right words.

Eleanore braced herself for more of her aunt's disapproval and ventured into another impertinent topic. "I'm afraid I couldn't help noticing your purchase in the store. It's unusual for a woman to purchase a pistol."

Lottie lifted one shoulder, then leaned forward and spoke in a conspiratorially low voice. "It's a gift for my brother. As cross as I am with him for abandoning me, I cannot forgo his Christmas present." Her lips parted in a mischievous smile. "Since he is almost always with me, I took advantage of the opportunity to surprise him."

Eleanore relaxed. Lottie's explanation made perfect sense. She opened her mouth to say as much but was interrupted by the arrival of their food. As the three women began their meal, Eleanore considered whether to have the heroine of her current novel purchase a gun of her own. With her thoughts lost in how that might affect the rest of the plot, Eleanore was chewing the last bite of their first course when she noticed that Lottie was still meticulously cutting her salad into tiny pieces. It didn't appear as though she had eaten a single bite. Was her lack of appetite due to her illness or the worries resurrected by Eleanore's questions?

If the cause were the former, there was little Eleanore could do, but if it were the latter, surely, there was some way she could lighten the mood. "Do you enjoy reading, Miss Berdan?"

"I do, but I'm afraid what I read isn't very impressive. Or at least there are some who would disapprove."

Aunt Gladys frowned. "What do you mean? How can anyone disapprove of reading?"

"I must confess, the only reading that interests me is fiction." A new sparkle lit her eyes. "I especially enjoy mystery novels."

Eleanore gasped. "Oh, but I adore mysteries. Do you have any favorite authors?"

Lottie grinned and leaned forward. "Wilkie Collins and, of course, Anna Katharine Green. But lately, I've discovered a new author who's become my favorite. His name is E. L. Martin. Have you heard of him?"

Eleanore fought not to allow the surprised delight in her expression. Never before had she met a fan of her own writing. She didn't dare glance at Aunt Gladys, the sole keeper of her secret. "Yes, I've read all of Martin's books. Which is your favorite?"

Lottie's mouth quirked to one side as her gray-blue eyes drifted up and to her left. "That's a difficult question, but I believe I must say it was his latest that impressed me the most. It was so realistic the way he used the banker's secrets to bring him down." Her eyes took on a hard gleam that sent a chill through Eleanore. "Secrets truly are the Achilles' heel of powerful people."

Eleanore wanted to ask what she meant by that, but their next course arrived, and before she could resume their conversation, Lottie spoke. "Have you been to the hotel's library yet?"

Eleanore shook her head. "I'm afraid Father has kept us too busy, though I do hope to visit soon."

"If you're not otherwise engaged, I would be honored to join you there tomorrow after breakfast. Perhaps at about ten o'clock? We can search the titles for any mysteries we have not yet read. What do you say?"

Eleanore grinned. Such an invitation wouldn't be made by someone planning to end their life prematurely. All worry in that regard melted from her mind. "That sounds marvelous."

As Eleanore enjoyed her sea bass, Lottie again pushed food around her plate. The woman's certainty that no other physician could help her left Eleanore with only one recourse. She must enlist Father's help in locating Lottie's brother and urging his swift reunion with his sister.

~

*A*fter an uneventful trip back to the Hotel del Coronado, Eleanore and her aunt left Lottie waiting for the elevator and continued to their suite. As Eleanore had hoped, Father was still working at his desk.

"Father, I must speak with you."

He set his pen aside and gave her his full attention. "Yes, dear. What is it?"

Eleanore briefly explained Lottie's situation. "So her brother surely remains unaware that he has her claim tickets, or he would have arrived by now instead of leaving her to suffer."

"Whatever has any of this to do with me?"

"I'd like you to hire an investigator to track down her brother and inform him of her situation so that he might hasten his reunion with her, or in the very least, have her claim tickets sent ahead." The thought of Lottie Berdan's distress ought to be enough to persuade him of the wisdom in Eleanore's plan.

But her father scowled. "May I conclude from your

request that this woman is of modest means and has no other acquaintance at this hotel?"

"Yes, but—"

"I won't waste resources on a stranger, Eleanore. You said the young woman told you her brother would arrive soon. If she can be patient, surely, you can be." He returned his attention to the papers on his desk before adding, "And I don't want you associating with women of questionable background. We can't afford any hint of scandal with James so near to proposing."

The rebuke stung. She'd expected resistance, but she hadn't anticipated her father's outright dismissal. And his disapproval of her association with Lottie only added fuel to her determination. He hadn't even asked her name, only the details of her social status. Lottie may be alone and poor by the standards of the resort's guests, but she'd been nothing but kind and humble in Eleanore's presence.

Still, she bit back further protest. Once he'd made up his mind, Father was as unyielding as the steel beams his factories produced. Instead, she retrieved the full sum of next week's shopping money from her room and slipped out of the suite before her dozing aunt could awaken and question her actions.

Clutching her reticule, Eleanore marched toward the grand foyer, her jaw clenched. She scanned the elegant rotunda for any sign of a familiar face. Thankfully, neither James nor Thomas was present.

Approaching the front desk bedecked in pine

boughs and ribbon, she cleared her throat softly to gain the attention of the gentleman behind the polished wood. "Excuse me, sir," she began, her voice steady. "I'm in need of a private investigator. Do you happen to know where I might find one?"

The man regarded her with a polite but perplexed expression, adjusting his wire-rimmed spectacles. "I'm terribly sorry, Miss," he replied, his tone apologetic. "I'm afraid I don't have such information readily available. Perhaps you could inquire at the local sheriff's office or seek out advertisements in the newspaper?"

Eleanore's heart sank at the suggestion. She had hoped for a more direct lead, but she refused to be deterred. Thanking the man politely, she turned away from the front desk...and froze.

~

Thomas stood transfixed by the pained look in Eleanore's gaze. He'd been passing through the rotunda when her conversation with the front desk clerk had slowed his steps.

Surprise flickered in her hazel eyes before she looked away and moved to walk around him.

"Wait." Despite two years of festering betrayal, he couldn't sever the bond he felt with her. Their lives had once been entwined with promises of love and a future together. Before his mother's illness and her father's cold ultimatum had shattered their hopes. As much as her presence filleted his heart, he couldn't ignore her plea for help.

She stopped and faced him, a storm of emotions swirling beneath the question in her gaze.

He swallowed hard. "I couldn't help but overhear." He glanced to where the front desk clerk watched them with keen interest. "I might be able to assist you. If you'll come with me outside?" He gestured toward the front door.

She bit her lip, cast a brief look at the nosy clerk, and nodded.

Torn between relief and dread, Thomas led her outside, down the stairs, and toward a two-story brick building that housed the equipment that created electricity for the entire island.

"This is far enough." Halfway across the manicured landscape, she stopped. "Tell me how you can help."

He squinted at the staring eyes of the hotel's windows. How many guests—or worse, staff—could see them right now? What would it look like to anyone watching? Would they assume he was assisting a guest or start rumors of impropriety? Either way, one look at Eleanore's squared shoulders and narrowed eyes told him she wouldn't continue to the privacy he'd sought on the other side of the hotel's powerhouse.

He clasped his wrist behind his back to keep from tugging her along. "I remember seeing a sign for a private investigator's office in San Diego." He drew in a breath, praying he wouldn't regret this. "I can take you there."

"Can't you tell me the address?"

He shook his head. "I don't remember exactly where the office was, only generally. But I'm sure I could find the location for you with little trouble." He offered a rueful smile. "You know I'm better at finding things than remembering them."

Her own lips started upward, then slammed down. "Thomas, I appreciate your offer, but Father would be furious if I were seen wandering the city with you."

He nodded. "Of course. I just..." He released his wrist to run a hand down his face. "I wanted to help. Look, I can go find the place on my own and tell you where it is tomorrow. I would have suggested that first, but you sounded so..." He shrugged. "It seemed urgent."

Her eyes softened, gratitude shining in their depths. "Thank you, Thomas. Truly."

Of course, anything for you. The old words stalled on his tongue. Too much had changed since he last uttered them. It was good she'd declined his offer. What had he been thinking to make the suggestion in the first place?

Eleanore turned to leave, then pivoted back. "You were right. The situation is urgent. What if I fetched my Aunt Gladys to accompany us?"

His heart lifted against his better judgment. "Do you think she'd agree?" Or was the older woman's opinion of Thomas in line with her brother's disdain?

Eleanore nodded vigorously. "I do. Wait here."

Before he could reply, she'd sped back toward the hotel, disappearing through the front door moments later.

Slowly, he crossed the distance to the driveway in front of the hotel. Should he order a carriage brought around to carry them to the hotel's train stop, or would the women prefer to walk the short distance? How would he explain getting into the conveyance with them? He was still debating the decision when Eleanore and her aunt exited the hotel.

Would the elder woman recognize him from her frequent visits to her brother's New York home? What would she make of his presence here? Would she reject his offer of help? Thomas braced himself.

Eleanore stopped before him. "Aunt Gladys, this is the bellboy who's agreed to take us to the investigator's office. Mr. Harding, this is my aunt, Miss Gladys Wainright."

The older woman barely glanced at him. "Your assistance is most appreciated, Mr. Harding. Shall we be off?" Without waiting for his response, Miss Wainright began striding toward the station with purpose.

Eleanore huffed and sent him an apologetic look. "Don't take it personally. She's unhappy with my plan." She squared her shoulders and hurried after her aunt.

Thomas swallowed a chuckle as he dashed to catch up. Despite her more refined appearance and manners, Eleanore was stubborn as ever and still ruffling feathers.

~

*E*leanore sat stiffly on the wooden bench of the open-air train car, her hands folded primly in her lap. Since her last ride in the conveyance, silk poinsettias had been tacked into the corners, a nod to the impending holiday. The clatter of wheels against tracks drowned out the rhythmic slap of ocean waves and any cries by the seagulls overhead. Aunt Gladys occupied the space to her right with Thomas on the bench across from them.

Aunt Gladys turned her face into the strong breeze flowing through the open windows. "I must say, this train to the ferry is delightful."

"It is convenient." Eleanore's gaze strayed to Thomas, whose attention was seemingly fixed on the passing scenery. What was he thinking of? Did memories from the past plague him as they did her? If so, his profile gave no hint of his feelings on the subject.

Aunt Gladys continued. "I admit, I was hesitant when your father invited me to join you on this trip. I'd never heard of the Hotel del Coronado, but I have been pleasantly surprised since our arrival." She straightened, her gaze caught on something outside the window. "Oh, look! There's the ostrich farm I've heard so much about. We should plan a visit soon, don't you think?"

Eleanore murmured her agreement. Thomas seemed to be deliberately avoiding her gaze. Did that indicate some notion of guilt over his choices two years prior? Was that what had motivated his offer of assistance? She sniffed. If he thought helping her find an investigator could in any way make amends for shattering her trust—

Aunt Gladys interrupted Eleanore's growing simmer. "Oh, Eleanore dear, did I tell you about Mr. Mitchell's latest gift? Such a charming man, that James."

Thomas finally looked at Eleanore, a pained curiosity in his eyes.

She pretended not to notice and faced her aunt. "Yes, it was very thoughtful of him to send those potted pine trees after you mentioned missing your traditions." During their ride to the La Jolla sea caves, her aunt had bemoaned being away from the pair of pine trees flanking the entrance to her gardens in New York which she decorated each year on the first of December. Upon their return from shopping this afternoon, Aunt Gladys had discovered two small potted pine trees guarding the entrance to her hotel room. A note had revealed James to be behind the surprise.

"Precious little is more important than tradition." Aunt Gladys's wrinkled lips puckered. "Not that your father has ever understood such. Things were different when your mother was alive. The holidays were something to cherish. Each year, by the stroke of midnight on November thirtieth, her home was the epitome of holiday cheer."

Eleanore warmed with the remembrance of one of her few happy memories of Mother. "It was nothing short of miraculous how the Christmas season revived her."

Aunt Gladys's eyes sparkled merrily. "That house-keeper of hers was of the highest quality. She executed your mother's visions to perfection. I never could understand how your father let her go. What was her name?" Her aunt's brow furrowed. "Howard? Hastings?"

"Harding," Thomas interjected before Eleanore could force her tongue to work. His expression was pinched as he continued. "Her name was Martha Harding, and she was the best woman to have ever walked this earth. She loved Mrs. Wainright. She'd have done anything for her."

Aunt Gladys's eyes widened. "But how could you know that?" She appeared to study Thomas as though seeing him for the first time. "What did you say your name was?"

Thomas glanced at Eleanore, an accusation in his look that made her flinch.

She ought to have explained their prior acquaintance when she'd first returned with Aunt Gladys. Heat climbed the back of Eleanore's neck. "Aunt Gladys, this is Mr. Thomas Harding, Martha Harding's son."

Aunt Gladys snapped her fingers. "I knew you looked familiar." Her knowing look bounced between them. "Then you're the boy my niece spoke so highly of growing up. The one who—" She stopped speaking as though thinking better of whatever she'd meant to say. Her lips pressed together, and she stared at her gloved hands in her lap a moment before straightening. She speared Thomas with her look. "Quite the coincidence, you working at the Hotel del Coronado."

Thomas's shoulders squared, his gaze not wavering beneath her aunt's scrutiny. "It is."

Aunt Gladys's mouth quirked to one side. "I suppose Rupert is aware of your presence at the hotel?"

"I've made no effort to hide."

A strained silence ensued, and Eleanore searched for a topic neither would object to. "How is your mother, Thomas?"

Thomas's entire body flinched as though she'd punched him, and his expression turned mournful. "She died. Seven days ago."

The air whooshed from Eleanore's lungs, and tears blurred her vision. "Oh, Thomas. I'm so sorry. Your mother was always kind to me." In truth, Thomas's mother had been more of a mother to Eleanore than her own had been. It was one of the reasons his leaving had rocked the foundation of her life. He'd taken his mother with him.

For a moment, the bond of their lifelong friendship flashed between them as he held her gaze. "Thank you, Eleanore. It's been...difficult, but I'm managing."

Aunt Gladys's voice softened. "I meant what I said. Your mother was a rare treasure. Please accept my condolences and extend them to the rest of your family."

Thomas's gaze flicked back to Eleanore before he replied. "Thank you, but it's just me now."

Aunt Gladys voiced the surprise Eleanore felt. "You have no other family? But I thought—"

Eleanore couldn't keep the question inside. "What about your wife?"

Thomas frowned as the train came to a stop at the pavilion station near Coronado's wharf. "I have no wife."

Eleanore started to ask if that meant he was a widower, but Aunt Gladys caught her hand and tugged her from the train. "Hurry, dear. I can see the ferry, and it's already boarding. You don't wish to miss it, do you?"

What Eleanore wanted was answers, but she followed her aunt dutifully. Once aboard, Thomas was engaged in dialogue by a gregarious hotel employee, who seemed to be a friend. Meanwhile, her aunt began speaking with an elegantly dressed older woman to her right. Eleanore was too stunned to focus on either conversation. Several times, Thomas's gaze strayed to hers, but his colleague's gift for gab left no opportunity to ask the questions burning her tongue.

Four minutes later, the ferry anchored beside a dock leading to San Diego.

"Eleanore, Mr. Harding, I have wonderful news." Aunt Gladys gained their attention with a grin and gestured toward her new friend. "This is Mrs. Margaret

Thompson, who lives here in San Diego. She knows exactly the office we're looking for and has agreed to show us the way. Which means, you, Mr. Harding, are at liberty to spend your afternoon break however you like."

Aunt Gladys beamed as Eleanore's stomach sank.

"Fantastic!" Thomas's friend declared. "That means you're free to join me and the boys."

Was it her imagination, or did Thomas's smile seem forced as he bid them farewell? Moments later, he disappeared into the crowd without a glance back.

Eleanore boarded a streetcar behind her aunt and Mrs. Thompson. It was just as well. What did it matter whether Thomas had married or not? He'd left her and never looked back. As he had today.

She ought to do the same.

CHAPTER 4

*T*homas spent less than an hour with his rowdy coworkers before making his excuses and returning to the hotel for his evening shift. Being drug away from Eleanore had left him in a sour mood, though he should be grateful. Her demeanor had made it clear she held no interest in rekindling their relationship, and her aunt had made certain he knew Eleanore had set her cap for James Mitchell. The wisest choice would be to put her out of his mind.

The moment Thomas stepped inside the hotel, Clarence informed him Miss Berdan had rung for assistance. An hour later, he finished filling the bathtub he'd helped carry into her room. The exertion of lugging buckets of hot water from the shared bathroom down the hall left him damp with sweat. He moved to the door with the empty bucket and turned to face the woman. "Will there be anything else, Miss?"

"I'd like a pitcher of ice if that isn't too much trouble."

"Of course. I'll be back momentarily." Thomas pulled open the door to find an unexpected fist aimed at his face and ducked. "What—" He looked up.

James Mitchell lowered his hand from smoothing it over his oiled, neatly parted hair.

The deceptive move didn't fool Thomas. James had clearly been about to knock on Miss Berdan's door. How did James Mitchell of New York know the humble Miss Berdan of Detroit? "Apologies, sir," Thomas muttered as he straightened and stepped into the hall, pulling the door closed behind him. "Miss Berdan isn't prepared for visitors."

James recoiled, then raised his chin. "Ridiculous assumptions, boy." His voice dripped with condescension. "I have no interest in speaking with someone I don't know, let alone any unmarried woman in her private quarters. I'm merely stretching my legs and exploring the resort— not that I owe someone such as *you* an explanation."

"I meant no offense, sir." Thomas flushed. Clearly, he'd misread the situation. "I thought—"

"I know exactly what your low-bred mind supposed. Such unfounded gossip could sully a good woman's name." James leaned forward in a clear attempt to remind Thomas of the extra two inches James had on him. "Keep them to yourself if you know what's good for you."

Thomas gritted his teeth against the urge to fight back. James Mitchell didn't scare him, but he needed this job. It was the first step toward his dream. He swallowed his pride. "Yes, sir. My apologies. It won't happen again."

With that, James turned on his heel and strode away.

From what little Thomas had witnessed of their interactions, James had maintained the behavior of a perfect gentleman around Eleanore. The woman he'd once known wouldn't want anything to do with a man who treated those he considered beneath him as James had just treated Thomas. She couldn't know about this side of him. But would she listen if Thomas tried to warn her?

~

The afternoon sun bathed the bay in a warm, honeyed light as Thomas and Clarence Blackwood, the hotel's chief clerk, rowed out into the bay for their afternoon fishing. They reached their favorite spot, and Clarence set anchor before they cast their lines. The gentle sway of the boat labored to release Thomas from his worries about James Mitchell and Eleanore.

A while later, Thomas's gaze fell upon a newlywed couple strolling hand in hand along the shore. Their laughter floated across the water. "Aren't they the guests who checked in yesterday?"

Clarence followed his gaze to where the two had stopped to hold each other close. "Sure are. They said they'd been married the day before." He laughed. "Not that anyone needed to tell me they were newly wed. The beauty of their love is written all over their faces."

"You always seem happier after a newlywed couple checks in."

"Who wouldn't be? Love like that can't help brightening the life of everyone who sees it."

Thomas studied his unmarried friend. "If I didn't know better, I'd say you sound a little lovesick yourself."

Clarence scrunched his nose. "I always hated that saying. Love doesn't make you sick. It makes you feel better about everything—even the hard days."

Thomas straightened. "So there is someone. Who?"

Clarence's face reddened. "What, me? Have a sweetheart?" He shook his head, his expression falling. "Only in my dreams."

Thomas adjusted his position on the boat's hard bench. "More like a nightmare."

Clarence eyed him. "What do you mean?"

A tug on his line made Thomas squint at the sparkling water, checking for signs of a catch. "Love may burn bright in the beginning, but it's like a match —quickly fading and easily snuffed by the slightest breeze of difficulty. Romantic love isn't reliable. You need something greater—a true, lasting passion to push you through life's trials."

Clarence raised one arm. "Then what, pray tell, is your great passion, oh wise bellboy?"

Thomas chuckled and shoved his friend's shoulder. "I have one. I'm not going to be a bellboy forever."

"Oh really? Do tell."

Thomas sobered. "I want to own a sanitarium someday."

Clarence whistled. "I didn't realize my friend was a secret tycoon. Say, have I mentioned I could use a loan to—"

"Ha, ha." Following another tug on his line, Thomas began a slow game of pull and drag with the fish he was now certain had taken his bait. "I'm serious. But I don't want some big fancy place like The Del. I want my sanitarium to serve people of all classes."

Clarence gave him a knowing look. "People like your mother."

"Exactly." Without the bribe he'd accepted from Rupert Wainright, Mother would have died that next winter in New York. At least, that was what the doctors had warned her to expect when they'd diagnosed her with consumption on the same day he'd declared his love to Eleanore. The doctors told Mother that moving to a more temperate climate was her only hope, but she'd had no money for travel. Even if she'd spent her last penny of savings to reach California, she'd have had nothing left to live on, and no one would hire a woman with consumption. "Everyone should have access to the medical care they need, regardless of their social status or ability to pay."

Clarence made a noise in his throat. "That's a nice notion, but last I checked, doctors need to eat, and sanitariums don't build themselves for free."

Thomas finally freed his catch from the water and lowered its flopping body into the net Clarence held out for him. "I'm not naive to the expense involved." He removed the hook from the fish's mouth, baited it, and cast it back into the bay. "I just think there must be a better way. My mother worked hard her entire life, but when she needed help from those she'd served..." He couldn't voice the sickening truth.

"That's just the way it is, my friend. The man who labored to earn his money doesn't usually see any good reason to give it away."

"It's a good thing God doesn't think that way."

Clarence frowned. "What do you mean?"

"If God left it up to us to earn His love and forgiveness, we'd all be damned." Thomas felt the passion build in his chest. "He had it all, up there in heaven. The Trinity, power, everything. Yet He gave that up to come be a human on this miserable earth. And not only that, He died for the sins we'd committed. He gave everything for us."

"So now you're Jesus?"

Thomas laughed at his friend's obvious teasing. "Of course not. But my mother lived twenty-one months longer in San Diego than she would have in New York. She found joy here despite her illness. I just want to provide that same gift to others. To offer them a place of healing and respite, regardless of their station in life." And without sacrificing their dignity and heart, the way Thomas had been forced to.

Clarence shoved Thomas's shoulder gently. "You've got some big dreams, friend."

In the silence that followed, his thoughts drifted to another suffering woman. "Have you spoken with Miss Berdan lately? I know she keeps saying her brother, the physician, is coming, but I'm worried she's refusing to see a doctor for financial reasons." Thomas scratched the back of his neck. "She's made some strange requests over the past few days. An empty pint bottle, a sponge, alcohol, and matches. She said she wanted to burn some papers in the fireplace." He moved his line to another spot where there seemed to be more bugs on the water's surface. "I didn't see what she burned, but what if the papers were unpaid receipts? I knew a man who did that once, mistakenly believing he wouldn't have to pay if there was no evidence of his debt."

Clarence began reeling in his own fish. "As a matter of fact, when I learned of her requests for wine and whiskey, I made a point of speaking with her about finances. It didn't sit right with me, her showing up alone and ill. I wondered whether she had the funds to pay for her stay and expenses at the hotel." He nestled his catch in the net at the bottom of their boat. "I have to give her credit for being honest about not having as much on hand as she'll need. However, she assured me that if I telegraphed for funds from Jenkins, Whitman, and Associates, they would see her accounts settled. In the meantime, I urged her to send for the doctor and offered to light a fire for her. She refused both, strange woman."

"I thought she was from Detroit. Why is her money handled by a legal office in New York?" And what were the odds Miss Berdan employed the same law firm that had managed Rupert Wainright's affairs for three decades? In all Thomas's years growing up amid the gossip-filled servants' quarters of the Wainrights' huge mansion, he'd never heard the name Lottie Berdan mentioned. Surely, the connection between the two guests was a coincidence.

CHAPTER 5

*L*ips pinched with frustration, Eleanore followed her aunt up the front steps of the Hotel del Coronado as the last rays of sunlight faded into twilight. The private investigator had given them no assurances that he'd be successful in hastening the arrival of Lottie's brother. Rather, he'd cautioned them that finding missing persons typically took days and often weeks, even with as much information as Eleanore had been able to relay from her conversation with Lottie. He'd advised them that patience might be the better course in this situation. Nonetheless, Eleanore had commissioned him to set out for Orange at once in search of Lottie's brother. She only hoped the decision wasn't a foolish waste of money.

Aunt Gladys led the way into their room and rang the bell for service. "If the maid is prompt, we should have just enough time to dress for dinner."

Eleanore paused at the sight of a tiny leather object sitting beside a slip of paper on her vanity.

Eleanore,
I found this on the sidewalk in San Diego yesterday
and thought you might want to add it to your collection.
Father

She lifted the small item and discovered it was a doll's shoe. Though her heart pinched for the child who'd lost their toy's accessory, she smiled at Father's thoughtfulness. He couldn't understand what value Eleanore saw in a tarnished button, a rusted screw, half a book page, or any of the other odds and ends she kept in her box at home. To him, the items were no more than rubbish, but for her, they ignited wonder. Where had they come from? Who had lost them and why? Where had they been before Eleanore found them? Each object had its own story to tell, and though she would never know the truth of any of their histories, she reveled in imagining what might have happened to bring them to her. Father considered her hobby harmless and not only didn't discourage her, but he sometimes contributed to it.

With a knock, the maid entered, and Eleanore tucked the tiny shoe into a drawer, silently promising herself time to wonder over it later.

Several minutes later, as Eleanore sat before the mirror, her maid secured the final pin in her hair.

Eleanore caught Aunt Gladys's gaze in the reflection. "You know, I think I feel a bit of a headache coming on. Perhaps—"

"Pish." Aunt Gladys tugged her gloves on. "You think I don't know you're making an excuse to stay and write?" Her aunt smirked. "You'd think a writer could come up with something more original and convincing than a feigned headache."

Eleanore bit her tongue to keep from pointing out how often her aunt employed the same ruse. The maid withdrew two necklaces—one diamond, one pearl—from the jewelry box. Something small fell from the entwined necklaces. "Oh dear."

The maid retrieved Aunt Gladys's emerald ring from the rug, dropped it back into the box, and untangled the two necklaces. She held them up with a silent question, and Eleanore tipped her chin toward the pearls.

Aunt Gladys stepped closer. "I'll manage that." She took the jewelry from the young woman's hand. "Thank you. You may go."

The maid left, and Aunt Gladys's concerned gaze fixated on Eleanore, as though she was trying to unravel a mystery. "Eleanore, dear, forgive me for prying, but I couldn't help noticing your demeanor around Mr. Harding during our journey today." She set the pearl strand on the vanity. The clatter of jewelry against the hard surface mirrored the tension that swirled between them.

Eleanore trailed her fingers along the pearl strand, avoiding her aunt's probing gaze. "What do you mean?"

"It's unlike you to be so quiet. Particularly around someone you know so well as Mr. Harding. I realize you've not seen each other since he left to marry that young woman in San Francisco, but I can't help feeling there's something you haven't told me." Her aunt draped the pearl necklace around Eleanore's neck and fastened it. "You were so stiff and quiet, almost...timid."

Her aunt was right. Eleanore hadn't been herself this afternoon. How ironic since Thomas had once been the only person who truly knew and accepted her for who she was. Or so he'd led her to believe.

Aunt Gladys's caring gaze met hers in the mirror. "Won't you tell me?"

She should have expected this. She'd inherited her unusual skills of observation from her aunt, after all. Eleanore would have been more surprised if her aunt hadn't noticed the tension between Eleanore and Thomas.

Eleanore dropped her gaze to her lap, the painful memories she'd worked hard to bury deep suddenly pressing toward the surface. "It's nothing, Aunt Gladys. Just an old matter." Even she recognized the hint of bitterness in her voice.

Her aunt's expression turned sad as she cupped Eleanore's shoulders in her gloved hands. "When we are young, feelings are easily misunderstood. Particularly in friendships of long standing."

The gentle understanding and compassion in Aunt Gladys's voice brought tears to Eleanore's eyes and a lump to her throat. "How...how did you know?"

"I may be old now, but I was young once." She turned Eleanore to face her. "Please, share your secret. Burdens are easier to bear when shared."

Like an ink bottle suddenly tipped, the long-hidden truth poured from Eleanore's lips. "It was so sudden, and yet it wasn't. I think...I think I'd known I loved him for a while but hadn't admitted it, even to myself. Then one day, I returned from a ride and remained to speak with him in the stables. We were talking while he brushed my horse and somehow found ourselves standing close. So close. And then he kissed me...or I kissed him? I'm honestly not sure."

"But you liked it."

Eleanore's cheeks warmed. "*Like* isn't the word for how it felt to kiss him."

"So what happened?"

Eleanore closed her eyes against the bittersweet memory. "He told me he loved me."

"And did you return the sentiment?"

"I did." Her voice cracked as tears dripped down her face. "He said he'd made an appointment to speak with Father the next afternoon. I thought he was going to ask permission to court me." He'd also said he'd wanted to marry her. She lifted tear-blurred eyes to her aunt. "But none of it was true."

"He didn't speak with your father?" Smile gone,

Aunt Gladys withdrew her handkerchief and offered it to Eleanore.

Eleanore accepted it, dabbed her cheeks, and blew her nose. She straightened, the tears giving way to the rock of anger that had been her anchor these past two years. "He did, but not about me. What Thomas had failed to disclose was that he'd already spoken with Father...about another woman and a position at a bank."

Aunt Gladys rubbed Eleanore's arm. "The woman in San Francisco?"

"After Thomas disappeared, Father explained that he had learned of a friend who owned a large bank that was searching for a trustworthy man to marry his sickly daughter and bring her joy in the few years she might have left. In exchange, the groom would receive a prestigious job at a bank in San Francisco, a generous dowry, and would be the sole heir to the banker's wealth. Because there were rumors the woman was also mentally unstable, the banker hadn't been able to secure a husband for his daughter. So Father suggested Thomas, and an agreement was made between the three of them." Eleanore clenched the handkerchief in her fist. "Thomas's appointment with Father hadn't been to ask for permission to court me. It had been to sign the final papers making the arrangement legally binding."

Aunt Gladys gasped. "No wonder you were so tense today. I'm amazed you accepted his aid at all."

Eleanore sagged in her chair. "Father had refused to help, and no one else knew where to find an investigator. I couldn't let my anger with Thomas cause Miss Berdan more suffering."

Aunt Gladys dipped a clean handkerchief in the washbasin and patted cool water beneath Eleanore's eyes. "Thank you for telling me. Although..." She pursed her lips in clear debate.

"What?"

"If Thomas gained so much money and that position at the bank...what is he doing working here as a bellboy?"

Eleanore sighed. "I have no idea." And the mystery had been gnawing at her since his first appearance on the hotel's front steps.

"Hmm." Aunt Gladys set the cloth aside and studied her. "What of your feelings now, my dear? I can see you're still hurt and angry with him, but do you also harbor affection for Mr. Harding? Or have James Mitchell's attentions earned your heart?"

"Neither." Eleanore squared her shoulders. "Love is a fool's game, and I have no desire to play the fool again."

Aunt Gladys's lips pinched in obvious concern. "Though I never married, I have seen the incredible joy a loving marriage can bring. I caution you not to harden yourself against the opportunity, should it present itself."

"God's love and the stories I weave in secret bring

more than enough joy to my life. If I can please Father as well by marrying a man he approves of, and who will open doors to society and business opportunities Father otherwise might not have access to, then I will be utterly content." Eleanore stood. "Now, I believe I must go or risk being late for the evening meal."

"You and Mr. Harding were close for many years. Should I assume he knows of your writing and supports it?"

"He knows of my writing, but not that I've managed publication. He was gone by the time I gained my first contract." Eleanore yanked on her gloves. "As for his support..." She chewed her lower lip. "He was the one who convinced me to pursue publication. But his actions of two years ago have since cast doubt on everything he ever said to me."

"Hmm." Aunt Gladys rose and caught Eleanore's gaze. "Have you considered that few high society husbands would tolerate their wives writing novels?"

Eleanore's stomach clenched. The thought had occurred to her, but she'd told herself such concerns were premature. James had not yet declared himself, and until he did, there was no point dithering over a choice that might never present itself.

*W*ith her hand on James's arm, Eleanore followed Father and Aunt Gladys into the Hotel del Coronado's opulent Crown Room. The architectural marvel had yet to lose its wonder for her. Each time she stepped into the sixty-by-one-hundred-sixty-foot space, her gaze was drawn to the thirty-three-foot-high, self-supported arched ceiling that curved into a dome at one end. She'd been told its exposed, cross-hatch structure was made from Oregon sugar pine. As usual, an orchestra's melodious strains floated down from ornate balconies, adding to the ambiance. New this evening, though, were the boughs of evergreen draped across the balconies' railings and the smattering of holly, ribbons, and poinsettias that added a festive feel to the dining hall.

Father and James assisted Aunt Gladys and Eleanore into their seats at a cloth-covered table before taking their own. Eleanore removed her gloves as the men promptly fell into discussion regarding the meeting they'd both attended that afternoon. Unfortunately, that left Eleanore free to churn over the conversation she'd had with Aunt Gladys. And the painful emotions it had stirred. Determined not to allow them reign over her, she forced herself to focus on the orchestra's lyrical performance.

A waiter served their first course, and still the men yammered on. As the servant departed, Aunt Gladys cleared her throat. "This soup appears delicious. Don't you think so, Rupert?"

The men paused to consider her aunt with surprise. Father's rueful grin was the first indication he'd understood her aunt's diplomatic reminder that the two of them were not alone at the table. "My apologies, Gladys. Have I told you how splendid you look this evening?"

Aunt Gladys responded with the type of smug smile only elder siblings could bestow on their younger siblings. "Thank you, Rupert. How kind of you to notice."

James shifted in his seat, seeming to study Eleanore. "That necklace is especially becoming on you, Eleanore."

She forced a smile and thanked him for the blatantly insincere compliment.

James must have sensed her dissatisfaction since, rather than claim his fork and begin eating as Father had, he leaned forward. "Tell me. How was your day? I believe you and your aunt spent some time shopping in San Diego. Did you find anything of note?"

Finally, a topic to take her mind from Thomas. "Actually, I've made a new friend. She's another guest here at the hotel. Her name is Miss Lottie Berdan, and we had a lovely lunch together."

Father scowled.

Something shifted in James's eyes as well. "Am I to understand you dined with a woman of unknown acquaintance? Do you think that wise? You know nothing of her reputation. She could be an impostor, a swindler, and a thief, for all you know."

Eleanore laughed. "Don't be ridiculous. She's a perfectly respectable woman in difficult circumstances. More than that, she's clever and shares my love for reading. We've made plans to meet at the library tomorrow morning to—"

Father's face turned ruddy. "You've what?"

James shook his head. "It's bad enough you've dined publicly with a woman of unknown repute. Don't make things worse by continuing the association." He lifted his glass of wine and took a sip. "Really, Eleanore, I thought you were wiser than this."

She worked to keep her mouth from hanging open. What was the matter with these men? "We're going to read novels, for goodness' sake. What harm can come from that?"

James set his glass down hard enough to slosh red stains onto the white tablecloth. "Novels are nothing more than a poor man's excuse for not working and a dull-witted woman's method of passing the time for want of anything worthwhile to do."

Eleanore reared back, James's words striking her as violently as a slap to the face. No. A knife. Straight to her heart. Her chest burned with angry words, but she couldn't form them into a coherent sentence.

Aunt Gladys laid her hand over Eleanore's. "Now,

dear, the men are only trying to protect you. Perhaps they spoke too harshly in their ardor, but—"

"I'm fine, Aunt, thank you." Eleanore forced a smile. "It's only that I suddenly feel a strong headache." She moved her napkin from her lap to the table and tugged her gloves on before standing. "If you'll excuse me, I think I'll retire for the evening."

Both men jumped to their feet, though her father protested. "Come now, Eleanore. It can't be as bad as all that."

Eleanore couldn't meet his gaze. "I'm sorry, Father." In her periphery, Eleanore saw his mouth open, but a shake of Aunt Gladys's head had him closing it again.

With gratitude, Eleanore escaped the Crown Room.

Once in the hall, rather than retreating to her room as planned, Eleanore was drawn toward the beach. Perhaps the soothing sounds of the waves crashing against the shore would calm her desire to storm back into the dining hall and proudly declare the truth of her secret profession. Would they dare call her dull-witted after she proved she'd fooled them both?

CHAPTER 6

Thomas scoured the moonlit beach outside the Hotel del Coronado for any hint of the guest, Mr. White. The sand was all but abandoned given the booming waves and roaring winds preceding a squall. Nonetheless, the man wasn't in his room, and this was the last part of the resort's public spaces Thomas had yet to explore in his hunt for the elusive guest. If Mr. White wasn't on the beach, Thomas didn't know where else to look. He scanned the shoreline, searching for the man who'd been eagerly awaiting the arrival of the telegraph in Thomas's pocket. Rather than the masculine form he sought, a distinctly feminine silhouette paced the sand. Silver moonlight danced along the loosened strands of her honey-blond hair whipping in the angry breeze.

Eleanore.

He faltered at the sight of her, a flood of emotions surging within him. Despite her betrayal and the passing years, his heart didn't seem to have received the message he'd shared with Clarence in the boat. Eleanore wasn't part of his life anymore. He'd grown wiser in their time apart and knew better than to trust in something as fickle as a woman's love.

Yet Thomas veered off his intended path, his steps carrying him toward the very woman he'd planned to avoid. As he drew closer, the tension in her posture and rigid footfalls shouted of inner turmoil. Turmoil that was none of his business. He should turn around now, before she noticed him.

He moved closer and hollered over the cacophony. "What troubles you, Eleanore?"

She whirled toward him, a flurry of emotions raging in her eyes as wild as the incoming weather. "Thomas. What are you doing here?"

He patted his pocket. "I have a telegram for a guest."

"There's no one else out here." She pointed over the empty shoreline. But her attention snagged on something behind Thomas.

He turned. A figure wearing a black sack cloak, with the head draped with a black lace shawl, stood on the hotel veranda. Thomas couldn't be certain it was Miss Berdan, but the figure's size was the same, and no other guest dressed as oddly. A gust of wind thrust the shawl up, forcing Miss Berdan to place a hand upon her head, revealing a flash of light near her neck. Jewelry? He wasn't aware Miss Berdan had brought any finery with her—another thing that set her apart from the rest of the luxurious hotel's guests.

"I meant what I said earlier." Eleanore's voice brought his attention back to her. She'd moved closer in his distraction, making her words easier to discern. "Your mother was a treasure—one I've greatly missed since..."

Thomas's heart clenched at the mention of his beloved mother, her memory a bittersweet reminder of why he'd left New York—and Eleanore—behind. It wasn't meant to have been forever. "If you treasured her so much, why couldn't you understand the choice I made?"

The moon was swallowed by a cloud, rendering Eleanore's expression impossible to perceive.

"Why couldn't I understand that you chose money over me? Must I really answer that?"

"That money gave my mother two more years of life she wouldn't have had otherwise. Was waiting three years too much to ask?"

She turned slightly, and the whites of her wide eyes flashed in the faint gleam of the hotel's electric lights shining through its many windows. "What do you mean?"

"Exactly what I said in my letter." All the old pain welled up, threatening to choke him. "I poured my heart out, and you couldn't be bothered to answer."

She gasped. "I never received any letter from you."

Shock laced her voice with the ring of truth. "You disappeared without a word."

She hadn't received his message? But he'd slid it beneath her bedroom door himself.

Before he could respond, another voice shouted from behind. "Thomas!"

Reluctantly, Thomas turned.

Mr. Babcock, the hotel's manager, waved for him to come. "I've found Mr. White!"

Frustration gnawed at him. If it were any other member of the hotel's staff, he'd tell them the telegram could wait. But Thomas couldn't afford to irritate his employer. He faced Eleanore. "I'll be right back. Will you wait?"

Eleanore chewed her lip a moment before nodding.

The tightness in his chest loosened, and he hastened toward the hotel. He made quick work of his duties, but when he returned to the beach, Eleanore was gone.

~

*E*leanore lay in bed, clutching the note tightly in her trembling hands. Thomas's hastily written words played over again in her mind.

I don't know what compelled you to leave, but please return to the beach where we may converse without fear of discovery and interference. No one will wander the shores in this weather, and I will wait for you beyond the reach of the hotel's lights. Though it seems important facts have been kept from us both, I pray you still trust me enough and care enough about the truth to take this risk.

Perilous though the rendezvous was, Eleanore would find no peace until she learned what Thomas had to say and weighed his words against Father's claims. She waited as the rhythmic sounds of Aunt Gladys's gentle breathing turned to snores. Silent as a shadow, Eleanore slipped from her bed and dressed without turning on the light.

The stroke of midnight had come and gone since she'd spied the slip of paper sliding beneath her door. She'd known immediately that it was from Thomas. Thank the Lord, Aunt Gladys had been busy with her nightly Bible reading and not noticed. Eleanore had moved as quickly as possible to cover the message with her skirts and, when her aunt continued reading, pretended to drop her brush in order to scoop up the missive.

She'd nearly jumped out of her skin after Thomas left her on the beach and she'd spied Father and James strolling along the enclosed veranda. All it would take was a glance in her direction for them to discover her out at night without a chaperone. And if Aunt Gladys wasn't with them, it could only mean she'd retired to their room. Which meant she'd discovered Eleanore wasn't there.

Reluctant as she was to leave without hearing the rest of what Thomas had to say, she'd felt compelled to rush back to her room. Thankfully, Aunt Gladys had understood when Eleanore explained her need to walk the beach and refrained from scolding her for doing so alone. Her aunt must still pity her for the men's earlier remarks. Yet it wasn't their words that echoed in her mind as she'd waited for the appointed hour to sneak away and see Thomas. It was Thomas's words about his mother needing the money and something about waiting three years.

She slid her feet into her slippers and eased the door open. Eleanore peeked into their sitting room. Unoccupied, as she'd expected. She tiptoed out, closing the door behind her.

Footsteps sounded somewhere out of sight.

Eleanore froze, listening. They were muffled, like someone pacing in their room on the floor above. She exhaled and exited into the hotel's courtyard.

Following the wide pathways that wove between the young exotic trees and shrubs dotting neatly trimmed beds of grass, Eleanore's hurried steps were hushed as a whisper. Still, her neck craned up toward the three stories of open walkways lining the garden's perimeter. Not another soul disturbed the night. Only the distant crash of waves and moans of the gusting wind stirred this inner sanctum of the hotel.

What am I doing?

If anyone caught her out and alone at this time of night, her reputation would be ruined. If they saw her with Thomas...

Eleanore stuttered to a stop before the doors leading to the hallway that would take her to the veranda and the beach beyond. Discovery would mean the end of James's attention toward her, perhaps the end of all hope for a match with any reputable man among New York's elite if word of her transgression reached the East Coast.

Despite James's ignorant, infuriating words and tendency to disdain those of a lower station, he'd never been anything but kind toward her prior to this evening. Had Aunt Gladys been right that James and Father were only trying to protect her and Eleanore ought to show more grace? Certainly, Eleanore had made her share of mistakes. And what of the doors James's connections could open for Father and any children they might have? Was she prepared to risk all her and Father's plans on the chance that Thomas might have a plausible explanation for betraying her trust?

Her fingers grazed the cold doorknob, then seized it firmly and turned. Whatever the consequences, she could not spend the rest of her life wondering. She must know the truth.

As strong as the winds had been earlier, their strength had magnified in the hours that had passed, nearly pushing her back inside as she exited the veranda and crossed the wide walkway separating the hotel from the sandy beach. She shivered as the frigid night air shoved through the layers of her ensemble, chilling her skin.

The hotel's windows still shined, and tall-but-feeble electric lights dotted the edge of the walkway, doing their best to push back the night. But the clouds had swallowed the moon, leaving no trace of its silvery light, and mere feet beyond the terraced land loomed inky blackness and the thunder of raging waves. Was Thomas out there as he'd promised? If so, how would she find him? Ignoring the skittering along her spine, she lifted her skirts, pressed into the wind, and aimed for the shoreline.

Minutes stretched into eternity as she searched the sand just shy of the foaming waves for any sign of movement amidst the darkness. The misty ocean spray drenched her skin and wilted her uncovered hair. Mud weighted the hem of her skirts. She must look a fright.

Something moved in the distance, at the steps leading to the beach near the northwest corner of the hotel. Eleanore paused, squinting against the night. Thomas?

Several seconds passed with no further sign of life.

She turned away, pacing south along the shore. How much longer could she wait? Memories of that long-ago afternoon spent waiting on tenterhooks for Thomas to come with news of his meeting with Father gnawed at Eleanore's resolve. Was it possible Thomas meant to betray her again? But why go to the trouble? It made no sense. Even in light of his betrayal, she could never believe him as cruel as that.

Thomas would come.

CHAPTER 7

*W*ith his uniform soaked by an age of searching, Thomas called himself every sort of fool for not choosing a more specific meeting place than the blackened, stormy beach. Was she even out here? Finally, a female silhouette emerged from the dark, striding along the shore. *Eleanore.* Praise the Lord, she'd come.

He rushed across the distance. "I'm so sorry I'm late. There was a spill I had to help with and..." His hands lifted almost of their own accord, responding to the aching desire to touch her—to prove that she actually stood before him, not as a figment of his imagination—but he came to his senses and pulled back. "Thank you for coming." The words seemed paltry in comparison to the intense gratitude swelling his chest.

She shouted above the roiling sea. "What did you

mean before, about your mother and a letter and waiting three years?"

He offered his arm and gestured toward the hotel. "First, let me take you away from the ocean spray. I've seen storms like this before, and the waves will soon overtake this spot."

Without hesitation, she placed her hand on his sleeve, and they fled the seething surf.

As they drew nearer the hotel, she slowed. "Someone will see us."

"Trust me." He tugged her forward, skirting Mr. Babcock's office and the pooling light that flooded the hotel's main entrance. He led her on until they reached the shadows blanketing the trees and shrubbery outside the empty, unlit Crown Room. Here, the night was far less black than by the ocean, but a glance around reassured him that they were well enough hidden from prying eyes. "You never received my letter?"

She pressed her lips together and shook her head.

He ran a hand through his hair. "I'm so sorry. But I don't understand. How is that possible? I slid it under your bedroom door myself, while you were napping. Didn't you see it when you awoke?"

"When was this?"

"The same afternoon I met with your father. Leaving the letter was the last thing I did before Mother and I left."

"But I wasn't home that afternoon. I'd gone to visit a

friend who'd received some bad news. Did you honestly believe I could sleep while I thought you were asking Father for permission to court me?"

Thomas's jaw clenched. "Your Father said you'd been plagued by a severe headache."

"But he knew I was gone. Why would he—"

"For the same reason he denied me permission to court you." Thomas's hands fisted at his sides. "Rupert has never believed I was good enough for you." Perhaps the man was right. Anyone worthy of Eleanore's affection would have waited to see the letter placed in her hand rather than cow to Rupert's demands.

Eleanore wrung her hands, desperation leaking into her tone. "No, you never asked. Father told you about the rich, sickly heiress in San Francisco whose father was offering wealth and an illustrious position to any reputable man who would wed her and make her happy for what little life she had left. You jumped at the offer, and my name never came up."

The air whooshed from Thomas's lungs. Was that what Rupert had told her? "How could you believe I would do that?"

She threw her hands up. "You were gone without a word. You and your mother. What was I supposed to believe?"

"That there was another explanation—one that didn't betray the promises I'd made to you."

"I tried." She wrapped her arms around her middle. "In the beginning, I refused to believe Father. I was certain he'd misunderstood. For days, weeks, I waited to hear from you, but it was as though you'd vanished." Her voice cracked on the last word, breaking Thomas's heart. "I started to wonder..."

When she didn't continue, he stepped closer and cupped her elbows. "What?"

"I thought perhaps I'd imagined our last day together—mistaken a dream for reality."

"Oh, Eleanore. I'm so sorry." Thomas tried to draw her into his arms, but she pulled away. He stuffed his hands in his pockets and kicked at the dead leaves littering the ground. "I never should have agreed to leaving that letter instead of speaking with you in person. But your father was so adamant. He said if I spoke to you again, even once, before the three years were up, he'd stop sending the payments Mother needed for treatment."

"What three years? Thomas, quit speaking in riddles and tell me the truth."

Thomas sucked in a breath. *Lord, please let her believe me.*

"As promised, I had arranged to meet with your father the day after we spoke. I couldn't sleep that night for planning and rehearsing exactly what I wanted to say to convince him that I would be a good husband and make you happy. But when I arrived at your house, Mother intercepted me with news from the doctor that the cough she'd been battling for weeks was, in reality, consumption."

"No," Eleanore gasped, her hand landing on his arm. "Oh, Thomas."

"He'd advised her to resign her position and move to a warmer climate immediately." Thomas chuckled bitterly. "What housekeeper has enough savings to follow such advice?"

"I was still in shock when your father beckoned me into his office. Without planning to, I found myself begging for his help. He was the only person I knew with the funds to help Mother."

Eleanore's fingers tightened around his bicep. "After all her years of loyal service, of course, Father would want to help."

Thomas worked his jaw, forcing the words past the lump of resentment clogging his throat. "That's what I'd thought too. But rather than show mercy, he issued an ultimatum. I could stay and court you, or take his money and move Mother to a healthier location where she might live longer and possibly be cured, in exchange for not contacting you for three years."

Eleanore released his arm to cover her mouth with both hands. "He didn't."

"He claimed the offer served everyone's best interests."

She dropped her hands, wringing them at her waist. "What? Why? I don't understand. Didn't you tell him that I..." She dipped her chin, her voice lowering to a pained whisper. "I welcomed your courtship?"

"He was convinced you were too young to truly

know what you wanted. He argued that if I stayed away for three years or until Mother died—whichever came last—it would give you the time you needed to be certain of your choice. He promised that if you still chose me after all that time, he wouldn't stand in our way." Rupert had been so smug, so sure of his assessment of Eleanore. Thomas should have known the man planned to resort to deceit in order to assure his success in seeing Eleanore married to someone he deemed more suitable. "He wanted me to leave without speaking to you, but I refused. I knew how much that would hurt you. When he agreed to let me leave a letter, I thought we'd reached a compromise, but I should have waited and given you the letter myself."

Eleanore stood silent and unmoving for several seconds, her chin still lowered so that he couldn't read her expression. Did she believe him? She must need time to think it all through.

He waited. And waited. Finally, he couldn't stand it anymore. "Eleanore?"

She looked up, tears glistening in the glow that reached them from the electric lights lining the hotel's driveway. "I don't want to believe you—that Father would deceive me so completely. But it seems the only reasonable explanation for your position as a bellboy. I knew something was wrong the moment I saw you here, but I never imagined this. Father has always spoken of seeing me married into the beau monde of New York's society, but these past two years, it's become an obsession. When Ward McAllister's Four Hundred list was published in February, Father set his sights on James Mitchell as my perfect match." She gave a wry chuckle. "Father's discovery that James planned to winter at the Hotel del Coronado is the entire reason we've come. Father arranged some business meetings to disguise his intentions. I don't think James has been fooled, though he hasn't objected."

"Why would he?" Thomas tucked a fugitive lock of hair behind her ear. "Even without your father's money, you are beautiful, intelligent, compassionate, loyal, talented, and so many other things that any man would be unspeakably blessed to call you his wife."

Eleanore swayed toward him. "Do you think so?"

"I know so." Thomas cupped her cheek with one hand and the nape of her neck with his other, urging her lips toward his.

Her eyes drifted closed, and her breath mingled with his.

Then she jerked back. "I'm sorry, I can't. It wouldn't be fair to James."

Her words sliced his heart. "Do the two of you have an understanding?" *Please, God, don't let me be too late.*

"He's made no declarations, but as I said, he's aware of Father's aspirations. And he's been nothing but kind to me." The tiny wince in her expression seeded doubt in Thomas's mind, but she continued. "I can't repay that kindness with the betrayal of his trust, and I need to speak with Father before..."

Her unfinished sentence gave Thomas hope. Yet he fought the urge to argue that he had declared his intentions and had done so long before James even knew Eleanore existed. She wasn't a prize to be claimed by the first comer. She had the right to choose her future happiness for herself. Besides, Thomas couldn't resent her for the very honesty and loyalty he had just praised. He swallowed hard. "I understand."

"Thank you. I..." Eleanore pursed her lips. "Well, good night." Without another word, she scurried away and disappeared around the ballroom.

He moved to follow after her and ensure she safely reentered the hotel, but a man's silhouette emerged from the shadows of the powerhouse several yards away, stalling Thomas's feet. Who would be out in this storm? The figure aimed for the same path Eleanore had just taken. Only the powerhouse crew had any business lingering near the brick building at night, though even they ought to have gone home by this hour. Why would the man not use the tunnel that connected the hotel to the powerhouse?

Curiosity aroused, Thomas followed the darker shadow. When the man passed beneath an electric light, Thomas jolted. Clarence. What was his friend doing here so late? He should be home in bed by now.

Thomas checked his watch and winced. It was well past the time he'd arranged to meet another bellboy at the wharf for a ride across the bay in the bellboy's family boat. If Thomas didn't rush, they'd no doubt leave without him.

He looked to where Clarence had been, but the chief clerk was gone.

Stuffing his watch back into his pocket along with his questions, Thomas turned and set out at a jog. The train didn't run this late, and it would be a long run to the wharf. He'd be feeling this late night come the morning. Yet as he pictured Eleanore's closed eyes and upturned face, he couldn't regret his choices. He only prayed her father wouldn't come between them again.

CHAPTER 8

*A*fter hours of tossing in her bed, Eleanore had risen with the dawn and begun pacing the private parlor that was a part of their suite. The moment Father emerged from his room, she'd attempted to confront him about Thomas's troubling claims. But he'd rebuffed her request for his attention with hurried promises of a conversation upon his return from yet another business meeting in San Diego. Despite her insistence that the matter was urgent, Father had dashed out the door, leaving her no choice but to wait.

Aunt Gladys exited her room. "Well, dear. Shall we proceed to the dining hall?"

"You go. I'm not hungry." Unanswered questions churned Eleanore's gut as strong as the wind had whipped the sea hours earlier.

Concern pinched Aunt Gladys's brow. "Is something wrong?"

"Yes, but do you mind if I tell you about it later? I need to speak with Father first." She couldn't risk tainting Aunt Gladys's opinion of her brother until he'd had a chance to defend himself against Thomas's claims.

"Very well." Aunt Gladys pressed the button that let staff know service was required. Moments later, a bellboy appeared—not Thomas. Aunt Gladys requested that tea and a tray of pastries be delivered to their room.

The refreshment arrived promptly, and as Aunt Gladys broke her fast, Eleanore stood beside the window and stared up at the crystal-clear blue sky. What was Thomas doing this morning? Was he working today, or did he have the day off? Why hadn't she thought to ask?

The tinkle of Aunt Gladys's cup against its saucer drew Eleanor's attention. "We've still a few hours before we're meant to meet Miss Berdan. What do you say we take a stroll to see what the storm cast up? Who knows? We may find some unique treasure to add to that strange collection of yours."

Eleanore smiled wryly. "I thought you told me to get rid of my collection." Unlike Father, Aunt Gladys viewed the odds and ends Eleanore cherished as unnecessary clutter.

Aunt Gladys sniffed as she tugged on her gloves.

"Yes, well, I dislike this dour look you've been wearing all morning, and I know how you delight in unusual discoveries."

Though her mind still wrestled over what had truly occurred two years prior, Eleanore's smile grew to a grin beneath the warmth of her aunt's care. She crossed the space and enveloped Aunt Gladys in a hug. "Oh how I love you."

"Oh pshaw. Of course, you do." She patted Eleanore's back and stepped away. "Now, don your gloves, and let's be on our way before I change my mind."

～

Shortly before eight o'clock, Thomas slogged along the sunroom in search of the guest who'd requested early-morning service. The gentleman was meant to be waiting at the far end of the sunroom, near the hotel's western oceanfront corner. However, no one lingered beside the distant empty rocking chairs. He ought to move quick, verify the guest was not where he'd planned to be, and return to the annunciator for further instruction. But exhaustion weighted his limbs. The lingering soreness from his late-night jog to the wharf served as a constant reminder of the events that had unfolded the night before.

Breakfast was still being served in the dining hall. Thomas hadn't dared peek into the room to ascertain whether Eleanore and her father were inside. Was it possible Eleanore had already spoken with Rupert? The man had always been an early riser, and Thomas couldn't imagine Eleanore waiting for such an important conversation. What had Rupert said? Did he confess the truth or concoct another lie? Had Eleanore believed him? When would she seek Thomas out? Should he seek her out? He rubbed his temple, willing the swirling questions away, but their haunting presence lingered like a specter in the recesses of his thoughts.

Thomas nearly bumped into Mr. Cone, one of the hotel's electricians, and muttered an apology. How had he missed the thump of the man's hurried gait?

The short, balding man clasped Thomas's arm and hissed, "There's a body."

Thomas gaped at the pale-faced, trembling man. "What did you say?"

"Shh!" Mr. Cone glanced around to be sure no guests were within hearing distance. "I said, there's a body. I found her while I was trimming the lights."

Cold washed over Thomas. It couldn't be Eleanore. It couldn't. She'd been perfectly healthy when he'd seen her, and there was no possibility anyone could mean her harm. Still, he had to know. "Where?"

"I'll show you."

Following the electrician's lead, Thomas hurried down the steps to the wide seawalk. Dread pooled in the pit of his stomach.

As if belying the grim discovery and even the raging storm that had blotted out the moon hours prior, a gentle breeze fluttered the slimy leaves on lumps of kelp and seaweed that littered the sandy beaches. The morning sun cast a golden glow over the beachside, but he felt none of its warmth as he made his way along the broad path toward the northwestern exterior staircase that bridged the gap between the seawalk and the sand.

There, sprawled upon the stairs with her feet pointed toward the ocean, lay Miss Lottie Berdan, her clothes wet, eyes unseeing. Blood pooled on the steps, and a pistol lay to her right.

A wave of sorrow washed over Thomas as he stared down at her. The bullet wound to her right temple spoke volumes. He knew she'd been suffering, but had her troubles been so unbearable? If he'd only realized the depths of her despair, perhaps he might have said something to prevent this tragic choice. Even Eleanore's efforts to hire an investigator had come too late. What terrible news they would be forced to share with Lottie's brother upon his arrival. A lump of regret clogged Thomas's throat, and tears blurred his vision.

Lord, why?

Thomas didn't understand how their loving God allowed such things to happen. Still, he clung to the unshakable truth that their God was loving and all powerful.

The electrician interrupted Thomas's mournful thoughts. "I need to report this."

Thomas wiped the moisture from his eyes. Mr. Cone was right. "You find Mr. Babcock. I'll find Clarence and something to cover her with." He shuddered to think of other guests coming across the gruesome sight and glanced toward the hotel's upper windows. Were they close enough that a child might see the scene from their window? He prayed not.

Minutes later, Clarence helped him lay out a canvas to shield Miss Berdan's lifeless form from unsuspecting eyes.

Clarence offered to stand watch until the coroner came.

Thomas shook his head. "You go. I failed her in life. Keeping guard over her in death is the least I can do."

Clarence set a hand on his shoulder. "This isn't your fault."

Then why did it feel as though it were?

~

After leaving word of their plans at the front desk in case Father returned early, Eleanore and Aunt Gladys had emerged from the main entrance and made their way southeast along the storm-tossed, seaweed-riddled beach until deciding to turn back.

Now, tranquil sunlight blanketed the shoreline as they neared the hotel once more. As they strolled side by side, their pace matched the rhythm of the lapping waves while they hunted for seashells and other treasures. With most guests still busy eating breakfast, she and Aunt Gladys had the oceanfront to themselves. Despite the serenity of the scene, however, Eleanore couldn't shake the weight from her chest.

With a heavy sigh, she tossed an unremarkable bit of broken seashell toward the lapping waves. Her gaze drifted toward the hotel. Would Father's meeting truly keep him away the whole day? How was she to bear the wait?

Movement near a northwestern staircase leading to the beach caught her attention. Thomas stood beside a large canvas draped over the steps like a shroud. Large stones weighted the top corners of the fabric, and Thomas stood on its bottom edge, preventing the sea breeze from revealing what was hidden. With his gaze fixed on the hotel, Thomas hadn't spotted her, but the grim set of his profile caused her mouth to go dry. Why did he look so grave? What was he doing? Was that a lump beneath the canvas?

Leaving Aunt Gladys, Eleanore hastened toward him. "Thomas, what's wrong? What are you doing here?"

"You shouldn't be here." Thomas's complexion paled. "Go back to the hotel."

After nearly kissing her last night, this was how he greeted her? She stiffened. "Last I checked, everyone was welcome on the beach."

Thomas raised his hands as if to ward her off. "This isn't something you should see. Please, just go."

The breeze lifted the canvas enough that Eleanore caught a glimpse of black cotton and the tip of a woman's boot. Tension seized her as she returned her gaze to Thomas's pain-filled one. "Is that...?" She couldn't voice her horrid suspicion.

Thomas pressed his lips together and shook his head. He wouldn't tell her.

She needed to know.

In a blink, she stooped and yanked up the edge of the canvas. The lifeless form of her new friend sprawled across the stairs, a pistol laying on the steps near her outstretched hand. The gunshot wound to her head, the obvious cause of death. But how? Why? Eleanore swallowed a scream as Thomas ripped the fabric from her grasp and settled it over Lottie once more.

He glared at her. "I told you not to look."

She glared back. "Whoever did this must feel the mighty wrath of justice."

"Whoever—?" Thomas's expression turned to disbelief, then compassion. "She did this to herself, Eleanore."

She swiped at the tears wetting her cheeks and rubbed them from her eyes. "She did no such thing."

Thomas pointed at the canvas. "You saw for yourself, the wound, the gun. It seems pretty clear to me."

"Then you're more gullible than I took you for, because Lottie Berdan made plans to meet me in the library less than three hours from now. Someone planning to commit suicide doesn't make plans."

Thomas ran a hand through his hair. "I don't know what to tell you. Maybe her illness grew worse in the night and she decided she couldn't take it anymore. I don't know—"

"That's precisely right. You don't know, Thomas. You didn't know her like I did."

"Don't make out as though you were best friends."

"I'm not saying that. But I did know her well enough to know that she didn't do this, and I'll prove it."

Thomas crossed his arms. "Just how do you plan to do that? This isn't one of your stories, Eleanore. The coroner will be here soon. Let him decide what happened."

Eleanore glanced back toward the hotel. No sign of anyone headed their way. Bracing herself for the horror, she stooped low enough to shove her head beneath the canvas despite Thomas's efforts to keep it pinned down. Taking in every detail, her attention snagged on something white nearly obscured by the fabric of Lottie's black sleeve. She snatched it up as strong arms wrapped around her waist and pulled her back into the sunlight.

Thomas set her on her feet. "Have you gone mad? If anyone saw you, they'd think you were tampering with the evid—" His words cut off at the sight of the cloth in her hands. "What's that?"

She waved the folded accessory in his face, feeling exactly like the clever sleuth in her latest novel. "A handkerchief. I found it tucked beneath Lottie's arm."

"You *have* gone mad." Thomas moved to stand so that his body blocked her from any prying eyes peering out hotel windows. "Give it to me, and I'll put it back before someone finds out you've touched it."

"There's embroidery. I can feel it." She began unfolding the thin cotton. "Mark my words, it'll be the initials of Lo—"—she swallowed hard—"of the true killer. Wait and see."

Thomas snatched at the cloth, but Eleanore moved it away, revealing the embroidered initials with a flick of her wrist.

And froze.

"No, it can't be." Cold sluiced through her veins as she stared at the letters *RGW* stitched by her own hand...for Father.

Aunt Gladys wandered over to them from the beach. "What are you doing over here, Eleanore? Is that your father's handkerchief?"

Thomas clasped her arm and thrust it against her side, then he shoved her from behind. "Go. Now."

She blinked back at him, too stunned to understand. "What?"

Urgency laced his tone. "The coroner's coming. You've got to get out of here."

She glanced over his shoulder toward the hotel. The hotel manager and a man who must be the coroner were rounding the ballroom at the building's southeastern corner.

"The what?" Aunt Gladys's question sounded like a

squawk. She looked from Thomas to the lumpy canvas to the swiftly approaching men. "Right." She snagged Eleanore's arm and pulled her away.

Still in a bit of a daze, Eleanore's steps slowed. "But I need to learn anything the coroner uncovers. I only got a glimpse of—"

"What you need to do is explain to me what on earth is going on. I've never seen a grown man so frightened." Aunt Gladys all but dragged Eleanore down the beach and around the northwestern corner of the hotel. "But not until we've reached the privacy of our suite."

CHAPTER 9

homas escorted the deputy coroner from the beach where Miss Berdan's body had just been loaded into a pine box and begun its journey to the undertaker. Eleanore wouldn't like that the official's initial assessment matched his own—Miss Berdan had taken her own life. Yet the discovery of Miss Berdan's purse on her person, still containing two plain handkerchiefs, a modest sum of money, a ring, and a small key, seemed further proof that the theory was correct. Any robber wouldn't have left valuables behind.

As Thomas entered the hotel ahead of the deputy coroner, the cheerful conversation and opulent surroundings proved a disconcerting contrast to the tragedy at hand.

The gilded-cage elevator carried them to the third floor, where Thomas strode down the hall, the deputy coroner on his heels. The official had estimated Miss

Berdan's death to have occurred in the wee hours of the morning. About the same time Thomas had witnessed Clarence outside the hotel. Surely, the two facts were unrelated. After all, Thomas himself had been outdoors well past a reasonable hour.

Had they both missed the sight of Miss Berdan's body due to the dark of the storm? Or had she died after he'd run for the ferry? Would the crashing waves have been enough to disguise the sound of a gunshot? They must have been since no one staying at the hotel had reported hearing such a disturbance.

The possibility that he or Eleanore could have been nearby when Lottie ended her life sent a shiver down his spine as he unlocked Miss Berdan's door and stepped back so the deputy coroner could enter. Thomas stood in the doorway as the official began meticulously examining the room, beginning with Miss Berdan's bed, which had clearly not been slept in. Her night dress waited in the open closet. The scene felt surreal, the weight of Miss Berdan's death heavy in the air.

After the bed, the deputy coroner's attention fell upon the items arranged neatly on the mantel over the fireplace. A black hat, penknife, quinine pills, two unlabeled bottles, and one wrapped in a strip of paper. He sniffed the first unlabeled bottle and muttered, "Camphor." Then he sniffed the second. "Alcohol...perhaps brandy." He removed the scrap wound around the third bottle and read aloud, "'If it does not relieve you, you'd better send for me. —M.'"

The deputy coroner pivoted to inspect the table. An envelope and small stack of paper lay on its surface.

The official read the envelope first and wrinkled his nose. "Bunch of nonsense." Again the man muttered to himself, and Thomas inched closer to catch his words, knowing Eleanore would demand a full account of this man's work. "Just her name written over and over again." He shook his head and snatched up the papers.

Thomas studied the deputy coroner's expression. Would there be a farewell note, some explanation for her desperate choice?

"Hmm. More of her signatures...Jenkins, Whitman, and Associates..."

Thomas cringed at the mention of Rupert's lawyer —the coincidence no longer bearing the ring of innocence.

"And what's this?" The deputy coroner moved the paper closer to his face. "'I merely heard of that man, I do not know him.' Hmm. Interesting." He flipped to the next paper. "Invitation to the hotel from Louise Leslie Carter and Lillian Russell—whoever they are." With a huff, he tucked the papers into his pocket and scanned the room.

His gaze landed on Miss Berdan's valise. Stooping, he removed the small key from his pocket, inserted it into the lock, and gave a twist. The bag opened with a click—handkerchiefs its only contents.

Thomas stiffened. Would there be another of Rupert's handkerchiefs found amid the stash? Had he been wrong to allow Eleanore to take the one she'd discovered? With concerted effort, he pushed the uncertainty aside as the deputy coroner shuffled quickly through the stack of folded cotton. Thomas glimpsed only a large *A* stitched on one. He was too far away to clearly see the others.

The deputy coroner returned the cloths to the valise and peeked under the bed but straightened again, empty-handed. He turned and stared at the pile of ashes in the grate of the fireplace. "Looks like burned paper." He knelt and reached a hand toward the mess.

"You asked for me, sir?"

Thomas jumped at the sound of Clarence's voice directly behind him.

The official stood, drew a notepad and pencil from his breast pocket, and crossed over to where Clarence fidgeted in the hall. "You're Mr. Blackwood, the chief clerk?"

Clarence squared his shoulders. "I am."

"Good. I understand from Mr. Harding that Miss Berdan asked you to telegraph certain parties regarding funds to pay for her stay. Is that correct?"

Clarence rubbed a palm against his thigh. "Yes, sir."

"And have you received a response?"

"Only this morning, sir. They said they would honor her draft for twenty-five dollars. Of course, I immediately replied that Miss Berdan had suicided on hotel grounds and that they should contact the coroner for more information."

Eleanore would be furious, but the deputy coroner seemed unfazed that Clarence had announced such a conclusion before his office had completed its inquest. "Very good. Thank you. Is there anything of merit you can offer regarding the young woman's death?"

Clarence shook his head. "No, sir. I know nothing about it except that she was found and Thomas and I covered her until your arrival."

"I see. Well, you may go for now, but expect to hear from the coroner soon. He'll want to interview you regarding Miss Berdan's actions prior to her death."

Clarence rushed away, an air of nervousness chasing him down the hall. Thomas knew him well enough to be certain Clarence had had no hand in Miss Berdan's death. But was it the mere subject of death that had him so rattled, or could his good friend be keeping dangerous secrets?

~

*E*leanore's heart pounded against her ribs as the chief clerk raced away. If he'd turned left instead of right, he'd have run straight into her. As it was, his heavy footsteps had given just enough warning for her to dive behind another corner when he'd first arrived. Her position, concealed from Thomas's view by a bend in the hallway, was risky, but it was the farthest she could be and still hear what was being said inside Lottie's room.

More commotion lured her to peek cautiously. Thomas and the deputy coroner were exiting Miss Berdan's room. She darted behind the same corner that had hidden her from the chief clerk and waited as footsteps followed the clerk's path. Then she inched out and risked another look toward Lottie's room.

Thomas stood alone in the hallway and drew a key from his pocket, preparing to lock the door.

Eleanore raced forward on tiptoes. "Wait," she whispered as she caught his arm. "Let me look."

Thomas shook off her arm. "There's no point. The deputy coroner has just finished his examination."

"I know." She gave him a rueful grin. "I've been listening. That man sure likes the sound of his own voice." Without waiting for Thomas's response, she twisted the doorknob, slipped inside, and yanked Thomas in after her.

He scowled. "Where is your aunt? You're going to get us both arrested."

Eleanore placed a finger to her lips. "Shh. You don't want anyone to hear us in here, do you?" Excitement trilled along her nerve endings as she whispered. "If you must know, my aunt is napping. This morning's revelation produced a bully of a headache."

Thomas's lips clamped shut, but his eyes shot pure fire.

She winced and turned away. She wouldn't let him

ruin her first chance to solve a real-life mystery. Especially since her new friend was counting on her to clear her name. Or at least, that's what Eleanore would want if she were in Lottie's place. After all, she'd only had one meal with the woman. Their conversation hadn't provided many clues into the mysterious lady's life, but it was enough to know Lottie hadn't planned on killing herself. She'd made plans with Eleanore and bought a Christmas gift. People with no hope for the future didn't buy Christmas gifts.

A tiny voice argued that Lottie might have been lying about the purpose of her gun purchase, but Eleanore shoved that voice into the darkest corner of her mind. It wasn't true, and she would prove it.

Hands on hips, Eleanore studied the room, noting the barren table, empty closet, and complete lack of personal effects. The deputy coroner had taken it all. Still, there might be something he'd missed.

She knelt beside the bed and peered into the dark recesses beneath it.

"There's nothing there. The deputy coroner already looked. Would you stand up so we can get out of here before we're caught?"

She glared up at him. "You said yourself the deputy coroner just finished his inspection. Who else has any reason to come in here? The maids can't come in to clean until the coroner finishes his inquest, and that'll probably take days. So quit worrying and help me look." She gestured to encompass the room, then resumed her inspection of the underside of the bed.

As she was about to rise, something between the mattress and bedframe caught her attention. Carefully, she extracted the torn parchment. Once the paper was freed, she sat back on her heels and flipped it over. "It's a newspaper clipping." The words *DOCTOR CONVICTED OF BLACKMAILING PATIENTS* jumped off the page. With Thomas leaning over her shoulder to read, Eleanore skimmed the short, undated article reporting that Dr. Malcolm Fielding of Chicago had been convicted of blackmailing his patients with confidential information and sentenced to two years in jail.

She turned her head toward Thomas. "Didn't the deputy coroner read a note signed by *M*? Do you think Lottie was one of this doctor's victims?"

Thomas shrugged. "I have no idea."

She tucked the paper into her sleeve and rose. Another scan of the room led her to stoop before the fireplace and dig her fingers through the ashes, searching for any larger fragments that might have escaped burning. She found two. One was nothing but a blank bit of paper. The second held part of a New York address she couldn't place. She lifted it for Thomas's inspection. "Do you know this address? It seems familiar, but—"

"That's the address for your father's lawyer."

A shiver traveled down her spine. First the handkerchief, now this. How could Father possibly know Lottie?

Thomas cleared his throat. "Eleanore, Miss Berdan instructed Clarence to wire your father's lawyer about funds to pay for her stay."

Panic raised her chin. "That doesn't mean anything. Jenkins, Whitman, and Associates are a large, well-known firm. There could be any number of reasons Lottie is—was—associated with them."

Thomas looked as though he wanted to argue, but he nodded. "Still, it won't look good when the authorities find out. It'll appear he hid a relationship with Miss Berdan."

"A relationship?" Eleanore gasped and jumped to her feet. "Now who's gone mad?"

"Have I?" Thomas's direct look made her squirm until she looked away.

"Fine. I'll admit it is strange that Lottie had Father's handkerchief, and that they share the same law firm is...well...also strange. But that doesn't mean Father had anything to do with Lottie's death."

"On that we can agree, at least." His expression softened, and he cupped her shoulder. "Eleanore, you need to accept that the evidence all points to Miss Berdan having taken her own life."

She jerked away. "Not all the evidence." She refused to believe Lottie had made plans with her she never intended to keep.

With a growl, Thomas raked a hand through his hair. "Have you considered that poking your nose into these matters might shine an uncomfortable light on your father?"

"Of course, but since he didn't—"

"And what about us?"

Eleanore's argument stilled on her tongue. What did he mean?

"The deputy coroner estimated Lottie's death occurred around the time that you and I were outside the hotel."

Eleanore gasped and covered her mouth with her palm.

"If this inquiry spreads further...I could lose my job, and your reputation will be ruined."

"Only if someone saw us and reports it."

"Which they're not likely to do if we're just a young couple seeking a bit of scandalous privacy. But if the officials start asking questions about where everyone was that night...even if no one saw us, are you prepared to lie to an officer of the law?"

Heat welled in her chest, and she clenched her fists. "What would you have me do? An innocent woman has been murdered, and you want me to rate my reputation higher?" She stepped backward. "I'm sorry if you lose your job, Thomas. Truly. But you can't ask me to let this go." She whirled toward the door, needing to escape the suddenly stifling confines of Lottie's room.

"Then you leave me no choice." Thomas's voice froze her with her hand on the doorknob.

She glanced back, a weight pooling in her stomach. "What do you mean?"

He held out his hand. "Give me the papers and the handkerchief. It's time to tell the coroner about them and your father's connection to Miss Berdan."

"I told you, there is no connection. It's just a coincidence."

"That's for the coroner to decide. Not you."

Ice sluiced over her with Thomas's firm declaration. But the coroner didn't know Father the way she did. He might assume that Father had something to do with Lottie's death when Eleanore knew that to be impossible. "You can't." Her voice broke as tears welled in her eyes.

His own eyes teared up. "I have to." His tone begged her to understand, and she did. This was his chance to have revenge on the man who'd wronged him two years prior. Because no matter how she'd wanted to deny it, Thomas's story about Father's ultimatum rang true. And now Thomas was going to see Father jailed for something he didn't do.

"Thomas, please." She searched his eyes for any hint of softening but found none. "At least let me speak with Father. Let me find out the truth and then, I promise, we'll tell the coroner."

He clenched his jaw.

She closed the space between them, taking his cheeks in her hands. "Please, for me."

He remained stiff as a statue for several seconds before his eyes shuttered with a ragged exhale. "All right. You have until dinner is over." He raised his gaze to hers. "But if you or your father haven't told the coroner by then, I will."

CHAPTER 10

$\mathcal{I}$n the quiet of their private parlor room, Eleanore checked her time piece. Nearly two in the afternoon. Three hours since she'd sent word of Lottie's death to the private investigator and still no reply. She'd been clear in her note that Lottie's death effected no change on Eleanore's desire to locate Lottie's brother. The physician might be able to shed light on who would wish his sister harm. If nothing else, he was needed to collect his sister's body. She frowned. Perhaps the investigator had not been in his office when the message was delivered.

She jumped to her feet and paced. How much longer would Father be? Surely, his meeting would not last the entire day. Aunt Gladys had long since woken, dressed, and left for the noon meal after Eleanore insisted she wasn't hungry. How could she eat with so many unanswered questions churning her gut?

After considerable debate, Eleanore had decided that confronting Father about Thomas first was wisest. Once Father perceived his connection to Lottie had been uncovered and that she was now dead...well, Eleanore couldn't predict how he would respond. But the shocking death of someone one knew and possibly cared for was likely to render anyone unable to speak coherently.

Footsteps sounded just outside the room. Aunt Gladys returned? Or Father? The doorknob twisted, and Eleanore dropped to the edge of the nearest chair, her hands clasped tight within the folds of her skirt. Heart pounding, she held her breath as the door swung inward.

Father paused in the entryway, a packet of papers in his hand. "Eleanore." He glanced around the room. "Where's Gladys?"

"She's in the dining hall."

He frowned. "Why aren't you with her? Are you unwell?"

"No, I've been waiting for you." She rose. "We must talk."

Father closed the door and turned back with a grin. "I knew he was close, but I didn't expect it would happen today."

Eleanore tried to understand Father's words and failed. "What are you talking about?"

Father tucked the papers beneath his arm, clapped his hands together, and rubbed his palms with glee.

"James, of course." His grin dimmed as he studied her, no doubt taking in her sobriety. "His declaration is what you wish to discuss, is it not?"

Eleanore shook her head. "Two years ago, Thomas left us without warning." Her voice faltered slightly, the remembered pain of his departure constricting her throat. She cleared it. "You said he'd gone to marry an heiress in San Francisco, yet now he works at this hotel as a bellboy. That makes no sense."

Father's chest puffed as he plucked the papers from under his arm. "And you think I have the answer to such a riddle? For all I know, the man gambled away his inheritance. It's of no matter to us, in any case." He started to move past her toward his room. "If you'll excuse me, I have correspondence—"

"I know about Thomas's mother."

Father stopped and turned to face her. "What about her?" His guarded expression revealed more than he surely intended.

Her chest ached. "So it's true," she whispered.

"What do you mean?" Father lifted his chin and narrowed his eyes. "Quit muttering nonsense, Eleanore. Out with it. What are you saying?"

She straightened to her full height, holding Father's frustrated gaze. "You forced Thomas to choose between his mother's life and marrying me. And you hid his letter from me."

Father's face grew red. "Is that what he's told you? The lying little—"

"Stop." Eleanore raised her hand to ward off Father's insults. "I'll not hear another word against Thomas. You may have fooled me two years ago when my heart was aching and I had no idea of your plans for my future. But I will have the truth now."

"*My* plans?" Father tossed the papers onto a nearby table. "You were as eager as I to come to Coronado and claim James Mitchell as your husband."

She opened her mouth to respond, but he cut her off.

"Don't deny it. You and your aunt spent weeks preparing your wardrobe for this trip and conspiring ways to secure James's attention. And now that everything is going so well, you want to throw it all away on a...a bellboy?" Father spat Thomas's position as though it were a curse. "I won't stand for it. So long as I have breath, you will not chain yourself to such a life."

Eleanore fisted her hands. "There is more to life than money and status."

"That's exactly what your mother said the day she married me and"—Father's voice wavered—"she lived to regret it." He clenched his jaw. "I won't let you make the same mistake."

Eleanore wanted to argue that she wasn't her mother, but the pain and regret in his eyes stilled the protest on her tongue. Perhaps now, with Mother's memory so close to mind, wasn't the time to plead her case. Still, Father waited for her reply. So she said the only thing she could. "I understand."

Father jerked his head and pivoted toward his room. But she had more hard news to discuss with him. "Father, wait."

He reached for the doorknob. "Enough, Eleanore. I have things to—"

"Lottie Berdan was found dead this morning." It wasn't how she'd meant to begin the discussion, but frustration shoved the words from her tongue.

Father staggered, placing his hand against the still-closed door. He turned, the color gone from his face as his stunned slate-blue eyes stared at her. His voice held a quarter of the strength it had wielded mere moments before. "What did you say?"

She stepped forward, softening her tone. "Lottie— the woman I came to you about whose brother was missing. She's dead."

Father reached for the nearest chair and sank into it as though his legs would no longer hold him. "How do you know?" Tears filled his eyes, blurring her own. She'd never seen Father cry before.

She reclaimed her own seat. "I saw her body." Eleanore pulled Father's handkerchief from her pocket. "This was next to it." She nibbled her lip as Father took the cloth.

He stared down at the white cotton with unseeing eyes.

His response to the news left no doubt. "You knew her."

"No...and yes." He blinked and seemed to see the handkerchief for the first time. "This is mine."

Unable to speak with shock squeezing her chest, Eleanore nodded.

"Where did you say you found it?"

Eleanore sucked in a breath and explained the morning's events on the beach, as well as the deputy coroner's suspicion that Lottie's death was the result of suicide.

An anguished cry burst from Father's lips, and he doubled over, holding his stomach as tears streamed down his face. "Not again."

Confusion and dread squeezed her middle. "Father, what do you mean?"

He took several seconds to collect himself. "Your mother...she—" He pressed his lips together and shook his head. "And now Lottie." He roughly wiped the moisture from his face. "I can't believe it."

"I don't understand." She reached for his hand, but he jerked it away. "How did you know Lottie?"

He stood and paced the room. "You need to understand, your mother was a cold woman. Not at first, of course." He paused, a sad, wistful smile lighting his eyes. "She was radiant. Like a sunbeam. An angel. Every man wanted her, but I won her. She was mine. Of all the men after her heart, she gave it to me." He frowned and resumed pacing. "But her parents refused to see... They ruined everything. We were so sure they'd have to accept me once we were married, but instead, they turned their backs on their only daughter."

Eleanore had no words. She couldn't understand how any parent could cut their own child out of their life.

He pivoted to face Eleanore, eyes blazing. "They put out the word, barring me from every home within their influence. My business was stymied for years. And their rejection broke your mother. My parents were long deceased, but I introduced her to the wives of all my acquaintances, who warmly welcomed her. I bought her everything she could wish for and hosted lavish parties in her honor. But it wasn't enough." He gripped the back of his chair. "Never again did she look at me as she had before our wedding. She'd turned dark and cold as coal. Though I loved her, she couldn't stand the sight of me."

Eleanore's heart ached for her father's loss. Only now did she realize none of her memories included her father and mother together. She couldn't even recall them dancing together at the Christmas ball. "But... what does any of this have to do with Lottie? How did you know her?"

Father shifted so she could see only part of his profile. "I've long dreaded this day. Prayed it would never come. At least, not until you were well married and firmly established among New York's elite. But now..."

Eleanore resisted the urge to shake him. "What haven't you told me?"

He pinned her with a hard stare. "You must promise never to breathe a word of this to anyone. It would destroy everything."

Cold pooled in her belly. What could be so awful? Could Father have had something to do with Lottie's death, after all? If so, how could she make the promise he demanded? "Please, just tell me." She forced herself to hold his gaze. "You can trust me."

He nodded curtly and pivoted away from her again. "It happened on a business trip to Chicago." His words came out gruff and halting. "It wasn't planned...I...we met on the street. She'd dropped her groceries, and I stopped to help her. There was no ill intent. But her smile... She was so warm and encouraging." Shoulders squared, he faced Eleanore. "I'd been lonely for a long time, and well...mistakes were made. I'm not proud of my choice, but...I'm only human."

Eleanore froze. He couldn't be saying what it seemed like he was saying. Could he? "Who are you speaking of? What are you saying?"

"Lottie's mother. We had an affair. It only lasted a week, but Lottie was the result." He grimaced, his voice dropping so that it was barely above a whisper. "Lottie is—was—your half sister."

Eleanore gasped, tears welling in her eyes. An affair was so unlike the fastidiously principled man she knew. That he'd been unfaithful to Mother and kept an illegitimate child secret for so many years seemed unthinkable. An ache filled her chest. For all her pride in assessing people, she'd deeply misjudged the two men she'd claimed to know best. What dark deed might Aunt Gladys be hiding?

Eleanore shook the hysterical thought away and forced herself to focus on the most important revelation. She had a sister. Or rather, she'd *had* a sister. The loss gutted her, pressing all the air from her lungs. For several minutes, she couldn't speak as tears trailed down her face. She replayed every one of the few images she had stored from her brief interactions with Lottie. Eventually, Eleanore pulled a handkerchief from her sleeve, dried her face, and blew her nose. "How long have you known?"

"Her mother contacted me when she realized she was pregnant. I made secret arrangements to ensure they were both cared for." His tear-filled eyes pleaded for understanding. "I made sure they never went without."

Except that as the child of an unwed mother, Lottie would have been an outcast, even among the poor. If only Eleanore had known. They might have grown up as friends even if they couldn't publicly reveal their sisterhood. "Did she know that you were her father?"

"I couldn't risk the scandal." Father smoothed a shaking hand over his thin blond hair. "Until her mother died last year, she had no idea. At that point, I directed my lawyer to continue the payments anonymously, see that she was clothed, fed, and housed respectably. But the clever girl discovered my identity." A begrudging smile curled his lips, and pride sparked in his watery blue eyes. "She came to Coronado seeking acknowledgment. She wanted me to publicly claim her as my daughter." The light in his eyes dulled as his expression sobered. "But I knew what that would do to your chances of a successful match. So I reasoned with her and she agreed to wait until your marriage." He stared at the carpet as he shook his head. "I thought she understood."

"Then she knew who I was?" Eleanore could only imagine the pain Lottie must have felt from their father asking her to remain a sordid secret and outcast while his other daughter climbed the final rung to the top of society. That Lottie had been able to keep silent and be so kind during their lunch together was a wonder Eleanore couldn't comprehend. "Did you know about her illness?"

"Only that it began as a stomach ailment almost a year ago. I paid for several doctors, but in the end, none of them seemed to know what was wrong. So she turned to her brother for treatment."

And now Lottie was dead. Eleanore would never have the chance to know the only sibling she'd ever had. But wait. "What about Lottie's brother, the doctor?" Father had said the affair lasted less than a month, but was it the truth?

"What about...?" Father's question trailed off as

comprehension dawned in his expression. "No. Lottie's mother was a widow when I met her. She mentioned an older son, but I never met the young man, and he certainly isn't mine."

Disappointment and relief battled in Eleanore's heart through the ensuing silence.

Finally, Father's shaky voice broke the stillness, though he appeared to be speaking more to himself than Eleanore. "I showed her the will, and she seemed so happy to sign the agreement. She was smiling." Eyes filled with pain and confusion lifted to hers. "She predicted you'd be married by June and spoke of spending next summer together."

"What agreement?"

"Lottie was to receive a larger monthly allowance beginning immediately and half of my estate upon my death. It was everything she'd asked for. I never thought that she'd..." He pulled at his hair. "Why? Why would she choose this?"

Father's anguish solidified Eleanore's conviction that he'd had nothing to do with Lottie's death, and his words added more reason to doubt the deputy coroner's assumptions of suicide. Why would a woman on the cusp of gaining a father, more money, and a substantial inheritance end her life?

Furthermore, his story explained both Lottie's request for funds from Father's lawyer and the burnt paper remnant Eleanore had found among the ashes in Lottie's fireplace. But if Lottie had seemed happy to sign the documents... "Why did you give Lottie your hand-kerchief?"

Father's face pinched with thought as he studied the cloth. "You say this was near her...her..."

"It was beneath her arm, yes."

He shook his head. "But I never gave it to her. The only person I've loaned my handkerchief to since we arrived was James, when you spilled that chocolate drink."

The recollection popped into Eleanore's mind. "James took all the handkerchiefs and promised to have them washed and returned. Remember?" She searched for a forgotten memory of her handkerchief being delivered but found none. "I never received mine back."

Father frowned. "Nor I. But James knows nothing of Lottie. He couldn't have given it to her. Someone from the hotel's laundry must have sent it to Lottie by mistake."

"Perhaps," Eleanore murmured, though her writer's instinct shouted that the odds of such a coincidence were suspiciously slim.

~

While the majority of the hotel's guests finished their evening meal in the dining hall, Thomas strolled beside Eleanore along the edge of the gently lapping surf, far from the electric lights of the hotel. Bright moonlight illuminated the whoosh and swish of the waves against the shore as he waited for her to share how Rupert had explained his treatment of Thomas. Instead, Eleanore quietly relayed her father's shocking confession that Lottie was the steel magnate's illegitimate daughter. The man was nothing if not diligent in guarding his reputation. Thomas struggled to imagine a circumstance that would drive the man to risk so much.

Eleanore finished her story and stopped walking. "So you see, I was right in my confidence that Father had nothing to do with Lottie's death."

His shoulders sagged with relief. She was right. "Rupert is a man of strategy and logic. Killing Lottie would bring far more risks than rewards, considering their relationship. And it doesn't make sense that he would go to the trouble of having an agreement and new will drawn up if he planned to kill her."

Eleanore resumed walking. "Exactly. Even if she'd threatened to go public before my wedding despite their agreement, Father cared for her too much to wish her harm."

"Which is why we must consider who else might have had reason to harm her."

"Not to mention means and opportunity."

Thomas stepped over a strand of seaweed. "Who else might stand to lose if Lottie went public?" He clamped his lips on the first name that jumped to mind. Eleanore would accuse him of being blinded by jealousy, and maybe he was. He certainly couldn't claim a level head where Eleanore's heart and hand were concerned. With the truth of Rupert's actions exposed, a new flame of hope had taken up residence in his heart. But was it right to ask her to give up so much to marry him? Was there any validity to Rupert's fears that Eleanore would regret choosing Thomas?

Eleanore stopped again and looked back at the hotel, now almost a mile behind them. "I can't think of anyone, except perhaps Aunt Gladys, but surely, you're not suggesting—"

"Of course not. But what about James?" Jealous or not, it made sense. "You said your father gave James his handkerchief. And if he hoped to marry you, he wouldn't want a scandal attached to your name."

She looked at him as though he was one shoe shy of a pair. "I told you, Father believes the maids misdelivered it. Besides, don't you think murder might be a bigger scandal than my secret sister?"

"Only if he gets caught."

She rolled her eyes. "Stop being ridiculous and think logically. James could have his pick of any number of New York debutantes. It's why Father went to the effort of bringing us here. He knew I'd have a better chance of securing James's affection with less competition around. If James knew of Lottie's ties to Father, he'd simply disassociate himself from us and that would be that."

Thomas grunted. She was right, of course. Eleanore had always been better at solving mysteries than he was. Even when they were kids, her keen sense of observation had made her the one others in the household came to when they'd lost something or wondered about another servant's unusual behavior. A small smile tilted his lips. Of course, her understanding of what she observed—particularly in regard to human behavior—had taken more time to develop. Misunderstandings and false assumptions had led more than one of their youthful adventures to an embarrassing or anticlimactic conclusion.

Eleanore's musings interrupted his memories. "I think we're looking at this all wrong. People commit murder for any number of reasons. It's likely her death had nothing to do with being my father's illegitimate daughter."

"Then where do we begin? I can't imagine why else anyone would want to hurt the kind, suffering woman I served."

Eleanore was quiet a moment. "*Why* is too big of a question. Let's start with what we know. Lottie was killed by a gunshot on the steps outside the hotel, most likely sometime in the wee hours of the morning." Again, her gaze turned in the direction they'd come from. "Since the gun used belonged to Lottie, there's no point figuring out who owns a gun. Which is good since I think every man in the hotel came prepared to hunt. And that means they would all know how to shoot Lottie's pistol." She wrinkled her nose. "The gun is a dead end."

Nostalgia warmed him as he waited silently while she churned over the details of the mystery. How many times had he witnessed her gift? Standing at her side once more was a feeling he never wanted to lose again.

Finally, she asked, "Who else might have been outside at that time of night?"

The question was like a bucket of ice water dumped over his head. Clarence.

Her keen eyes didn't miss his reaction.

"What?"

"My friend Clarence is the chief clerk at the hotel." He hesitated. Why was he bringing this up? There was no way Clarence—

"So?" Eleanore's probing gaze searched him.

Thomas sighed and rubbed the back of his neck. "I saw him outside the hotel after you left."

Eleanore's eyes widened. "Do you think—"

"No! Of course, not. It's just that you asked..." Thomas shook his head. "But he was coming from the powerhouse. That's the opposite direction from where Lottie's body was found. So it couldn't have been him."

Eleanore's eyes took on that speculative gleam Thomas remembered. "Still, if he was outside around that time, it's possible he saw or heard something that could help us. Maybe we should speak to whoever occupies the rooms on either side of Lottie's as well. The murder may have taken place on the beach, but there's a chance they heard her leave her room. That would give us a smaller window of time to examine."

Thinking of Lottie's room reminded Thomas of his strange encounter with James. "I see what you're saying, but I still think you're dismissing James too easily." He explained how James had inexplicably been on the third floor and appeared about to knock on Lottie's door.

Eleanore's head tilted to one side as she considered. "You don't think he was telling the truth about taking a walk?"

It was his turn to look at her as though she'd lost a few marbles. "On the third floor? Why not go outside? The weather was perfectly fine that day."

"I admit, it is strange, but sometimes people do strange things." She gave him a pointed look. "Such as linger beside empty powerhouses in the wee hours of the morning."

Thomas lifted his chin. "I'm sure Clarence has a reasonable explanation for his actions."

"As does James."

He crossed his arms. "Then maybe we should interview them both."

"But I've already explained why it wouldn't make sense for James to kill Lottie," Eleanore countered, her voice tinged with disbelief.

"And I'm telling you, I know Clarence. He'd never do something like this."

She faced the ocean in angry silence for several seconds. Finally, she released a frustrated sigh and peered up at him. "But we both agree Lottie's behavior and circumstances don't fit with the idea of suicide?"

He relaxed his stance. "We do."

"Then we owe it to her to uncover the truth, no matter who's behind it."

She was right. "Tell you what, I'll interview James to see if he has any connection to Lottie that we aren't aware of since I can remain more objective with him. You can interview Clarence."

She shook her head. "I see your point, but I think they're more likely to tell the truth to someone they trust."

Thomas considered her statement. "And the truth is what's most important here."

"Exactly."

CHAPTER 11

The crisp, late-morning air carried the faint scent of salt as Eleanore strolled with James around the wooden enclosures at the ostrich farm not far from the hotel. Father had intended to join them, but a last-minute business matter left her and Aunt Gladys alone with James for the excursion.

Prior to breakfast, Eleanore had sneaked away to speak with the women staying in rooms on either side of Lottie, but neither woman had heard or seen a thing that might be helpful. Which left only James as a possible source of information. From the corner of her eye, she studied James's profile. He was always so particular in regard to propriety. She couldn't imagine him having a secret relationship with any woman. Still, she had promised Thomas she would question James.

Her aunt stopped a few feet behind them, her attention captured by the farm's newest additions. "It's difficult to believe those large, rather homely creatures produce such adorable chicks."

Eleanore hummed her agreement as she kept pace with James, who seemed not to have heard Aunt Gladys's remark. Soon they were far enough away that Eleanore felt confident of a private conversation.

In a somber tone, she ventured, "I can't stop thinking about poor Miss Berdan."

James glanced at her with furrowed brow. "Who?"

"The woman whose body was found yesterday morning."

"Oh, her." James frowned and turned away. "Let's not think of dreary things when we are here to enjoy ourselves."

"I can't seem to help it." She repositioned herself for a better view of his expression. "I knew her for only a day, and we shared just a single meal together, but she had so much more life to live."

James pointed to where one of the long birds had tipped its head back and was jiggling food down its throat. "Look at that."

"Did you ever have the pleasure of speaking with Miss Berdan?"

"No." James strode farther along the fencing, forcing her to hurry to keep up.

"Then you knew nothing of her?"

"No more than what I've heard whispered among

staff since her death and the little shared by the newspaper." He stopped and took her hands. "Now, can we please be done with the subject? Miss Berdan's untimely passing seems to have cast a morbid pall over the hotel. I believe your father chose this morning's excursion because it would present a more cheerful atmosphere where we could enjoy each other's company." His expression oozed warmth, hope, and a pleading sincerity. "It's a shame he couldn't join us, but shouldn't we make the most of our visit?" He extended his bent elbow.

"Of course." Guilt pricked at her as she set her hand on his arm. James clearly knew nothing of Lottie, and Eleanore's persistence had befouled their time together. Father would be disappointed. With a glance back to where Aunt Gladys lingered beside the chicks' enclosure, Eleanore searched for a way to mend her faux pas. "Have you seen ostriches before?"

"I have." They continued another few yards alongside the corral as James shared about his first visit to New York City's Central Park Zoo. "There was a male bird that dropped to his knees and spread out its wings like a lady's fan. It began circling its long neck and head like a wonky carousel." He flapped his bent elbows and swiftly rolled his head in a hilarious imitation of the movement, causing his hat to fall.

Eleanore laughed as he retrieved his homburg and dusted it off before returning it to his head.

James chuckled, then paused and reached into his

coat pocket. He produced a small velvet box. "I've been waiting for the right moment, but no timing seems lovely enough to match your beauty. So I suppose this will have to do."

Eleanore's heart stuttered at the sight of the jewelry case. Just the right size for a ring. Surely, that wasn't what it held. James hadn't even declared an intent to court her—not officially—so he couldn't possibly mean to propose.

Eleanore stepped back. "James, I..." What should she say? Would Father want her to accept despite James's lack of official courtship? What did she want?

Thomas's face flashed in her mind. The memory of their near kiss filled her with yearning, but was it wise to follow her heart? He may not have married another, but he'd still chosen money over marrying her. Money for his dying mother. And his choice wasn't forever. He'd intended to return for Eleanore in three years. He'd expected her to wait. And what about now? Could he even afford a wife on a bellboy's salary, or would he ask her to wait longer? Assuming he still wanted to marry her after what Father did.

James was right here, ready to support a wife, and apparently, choosing her. James wouldn't ask her to wait. But could she be happy with him?

Before she could corral her twisting thoughts, James opened the box to reveal a stunning brooch. The gold pearl at the center of its delicate shell-like design glistened in the late-morning light. A surge of relief wilted her spine, but a twinge of unease kept her shoulders tense. His gift wasn't a ring, but the fine jewelry was too lavish. She couldn't accept such a present while her thoughts and feelings were still so tangled.

"Oh, James, it's lovely, but I can't possibly accept. It's too much." Eleanore glanced toward her aunt, praying she correctly interpreted Eleanore's wide eyes as a plea for help.

James's smile widened as he withdrew the brooch from its box. "Don't be silly. I insist. Consider it a token of my appreciation for your friendship." He stepped close, opened the pin, and slid it through the fabric near her shoulder. "There. It looks almost as exquisite as you."

"Th-thank you." Eleanore leaned away, the wood of the corral pressing into her back. She placed her fingertips over the metal shell. He'd said the gift was a token of his friendship, not love or even affection. There was nothing wrong in accepting that, was there?

❧

The bright afternoon sun flirted with wispy white clouds in the pale blue sky as Thomas and Clarence stood side by side at the edge of the pier. Their fishing lines trailed lazily into the sparkling ocean below.

The moment was so peaceful, Thomas hated to break the silence, but Eleanore would expect news when they met later that evening. Thankfully, the other men fishing along the pier had settled far enough away to allow a private conversation.

Thomas glanced at Clarence from the corner of his eye. Was there a way of easing into the topic? Nothing came to mind. Best to be frank. With his gaze fixed on the point where his line pierced the water, he asked, "What were you doing outside the hotel so late Monday night? I saw you coming from the powerhouse after midnight, Tuesday morning."

In the edges of his vision, Thomas saw Clarence straighten and glance at him before resuming staring at the water. "I was asked to deliver a note to one of the electricians." His words lacked their usual confidence.

Thomas adjusted his grip on his rod. The electricians usually left work hours before when he'd seen Clarence. "Was there some sort of trouble?"

Clarence shrugged. "Some issue with the wiring, I guess."

"What sort of issue?" Why hadn't Thomas heard about the trouble? Such occurrences were rare enough they'd be talked about among the staff. Unless everyone was still preoccupied by Lottie's death.

Seagulls wheeled overhead, their cries mingling with the gentle lapping of the waves against the pilings as Thomas discreetly studied Clarence's profile. There was a tension in his friend's jaw and shoulders that suggested there was more to the story than he was letting on. Still, his gut said Clarence was innocent of

Lottie's death. Whatever he wasn't sharing must not be related. He tried one more time. "You know you can trust me, right, Clarence?"

"Of course." Clarence smiled at him. "Now, are you going to yammer all day, or are we going to catch some fish?"

CHAPTER 12

*E*leanore slinked through the shadows outside the Crown Room, the crunch of dried leaves beneath her feet seeming to shout her scandalous behavior into the otherwise hushed night. With no storm whipping them, the waves were no more than a whisper on the breeze.

Something moved in the darkness.

She paused, trying to identify the tall silhouette. "Thomas?"

"I'm here," he called softly, and she hurried forward.

She came to a stop before him, the intimacy of their location evoking memories of the night they'd almost kissed. She shoved the thought away. They had more important things to discuss. "What did Clarence say?"

"That he'd been delivering a note to the electricians who were working late on a problem at the powerhouse."

"And you believe him?"

"I do. What about James?"

"He didn't know Lottie. When I first mentioned her, he didn't even know who I was referring to until I connected her name to the body."

"You're sure?"

Eleanore replayed in her mind the conversation with James. He had seemed eager to change the subject, but very few people wished to discuss death. The end of life was a subject many found frightening, especially those without a relationship with God.

Wait. Had she ever discussed the Lord with James? She couldn't recall the subject coming up. Nor did she recall Father mentioning that James attended church when he'd explained his reasons for wanting Eleanore to marry him. What if James was unsaved? Surely, Father didn't intend for her to be unequally yoked.

Nevertheless, the unanswered question was yet another reason she needed to return the brooch. Her earlier acceptance had eaten away at her all evening. The only thing that had stilled the nagging voice was a decision to return the brooch just as soon as she could find a gentle and private way of doing so.

"Eleanore?" Thomas's concerned tone alerted her that she'd been quiet too long.

"Sorry, I got lost in my thoughts. Yes, I'm certain James was telling the truth."

"Then we're back to where we started. Perhaps..."

Thomas hesitated, his brow furrowing. "Could we be underestimating her suffering? What if her illness was worse than we knew and she had regrets about her arrangement with your father? It couldn't have done her self-worth any favors to have Rupert deem your marital future more important than publicly acknowledging Lottie as his daughter. She couldn't even tell you."

"It's not as if she'd have had long to wait. James—" Eleanore caught herself before sharing her suspicions that the brooch had meant more than the friendship James had professed.

Thomas's eyes narrowed. "James what?"

"Nothing. I just think you're wrong. Father said Lottie was happy with the arrangement. She was being given half of my inheritance, after all."

Thomas crossed his arms. "Some people value things like love, loyalty, and acceptance above money."

"Father did love Lottie." Eleanore lifted her chin. "You didn't see him when he found out she was dead. He was devastated."

"You fell for his lies once before. How do you know he isn't lying now?"

Eleanore gasped and straightened to her full height. "I know. And if you can't trust my judgment, then I think we're done here." She pivoted on her heel and stormed away. With Thomas so blinded by bitterness toward Father, she'd have to find Lottie's killer on her own.

~

Thomas quietly called after Eleanore's retreating figure, but she either didn't hear him or chose to ignore him. With a frustrated huff, he followed discreetly behind her to ensure she made it safely back inside. Once the door swooshed shut behind her, he turned and stomped down the beach. Why was she being so bullheaded? For a few hours, he'd believed her conviction that Lottie had too much to live for to commit suicide. Yet they'd explored all the clues they could find and had come up empty. Was there anything that would convince her the facts were as plain as they seemed?

The sound of the waves crashing against the shore provided a soothing backdrop to his troubled thoughts. Eventually, the exhaustion of the day caught up to him, and he turned back. He needed to hurry if he was going to catch the last ferry.

As he approached the grand facade of the hotel, a petite figure emerged from the shadows near the powerhouse and darted toward the Crown Room. When the person passed beneath the lights ringing the hotel's front drive, Thomas recognized the uniform of a hotel maid before she slipped around the corner and out of sight.

Instinctively, he ducked behind a nearby pole that held the hotel's empty laundry lines and scanned the gloom surrounding the powerhouse.

Sure enough, a few minutes later, Clarence emerged from the murkiness, his movements furtive and hurried.

Thomas set off after him. His friend had lied to him.

Just like before, Clarence veered around the hotel manager's office. Thomas rushed to catch up, but by the time he rounded the ballroom, Clarence had vanished inside the hotel. Had he entered the lower level or gone up to the enclosed veranda? There was no clue directing Thomas which way to go, and he was running out of time to catch the ferry.

With a frustrated shake of his head, Thomas turned away. Clarence didn't know Thomas had seen him. He'd be at work in a few hours, just like any other day. Thomas could confront him then.

CHAPTER 13

That afternoon, Eleanore suppressed a yawn as she sat before the mirror in her room. Her wee-morning meetings with Thomas were taking their toll, but meeting during the day increased their odds of being seen together and word reaching Father. Shoving aside her fatigue, she checked that the pins in her hair were secure as she prepared to accompany Aunt Gladys to the hotel's bathhouse. Spending the afternoon swimming seemed a frivolous waste of time under the circumstances, but her aunt insisted. Since Eleanore had yet to come up with her next course of action in solving Lottie's murder, she'd agreed.

"Eleanore, would you care to share what's going on between you and your father?" Aunt Gladys crossed the room to stand beside her. "Don't think I missed that you barely spoke two words to him this morning over breakfast. I've tried to ignore the tension between you two over the last two days, hoping you'd work things out, but it seems only to be getting worse."

Eleanore's fingers stilled in her hair. She should have known her aunt would demand an explanation. Letting her hands fall, Eleanore sighed. "I admit, I've been reluctant to tell you. You think so highly of Father, I...I didn't want to change that."

"As much as I love your father, I'm well aware of his faults. I doubt there's much you could say that would shock me." Aunt Gladys's shrewd gaze studied Eleanore in the mirror. "This has something to do with Mr. Harding, doesn't it?"

"Yes." Taking a deep breath, Eleanore stood and faced her aunt. "Do you remember what I told you about Thomas leaving to marry the heiress in Chicago?"

Her aunt's lips scrunched to one side before she answered. "I remember the lie your father told you."

Eleanore gasped. "You knew?" Betrayal stole her breath. She'd never suspected her aunt of conspiring with Father to keep Eleanore from Thomas.

Her aunt's expression turned horrified. "Oh, not then, darling girl. No, I figured it out after you confided in me a few days ago. It didn't make sense for the young man to be working as a bellboy if he'd married into money."

"But you never said—"

"It wasn't my place to. What happened was between you and your father and Mr. Harding." Aunt Gladys cupped Eleanore's cheek. "Now, tell me. What really happened two years ago?"

Eleanore quickly explained Thomas's accusations and Father's justifications. "And Father's not even sorry. I think he'd do it again if he could."

Aunt Gladys nodded somberly. "I've no doubt he would."

Eleanore paced the room. "Then you must see why I'm so angry with him. Why I don't know what to say to him." She stopped to search her aunt's face. "He's my father. How could he lie to me like that?"

Aunt Gladys held out her hand, her eyes sad. "Come."

Eleanore allowed herself to be tugged to the edge of her bed. They both sat, and Aunt Gladys shifted to face Eleanore. "Your father didn't share your mother's full story because he didn't know it all. As a man used to shoving his feelings aside, he urged your mother to dismiss those who scorned them as he did. He couldn't understand the true depth of her grief."

"What do you mean?"

"Your mother's beauty and poise, combined with her family heritage and wealth, made her the most sought-after debutante of her season. Your father was but one of many men who attempted to woo her." Her eyes sparked with mischief. "Naturally, I mocked him for joining the crowd. I was certain he had no chance and was wasting his time."

"But you've always said your friends were heart-broken when Father married Mother."

"True. But we were of a different class. My own father was a humble factory owner. Not poor, but not rich by any means. Therefore, our family had no place in New York's high society. Even your father's increasing wealth wasn't enough to gain him a foothold among that lot. He was considered 'new money,' and those who'd reigned over New York for generations had no intention of muddying their lineage with families of questionable heritage."

Eleanore crossed her arms. "Father told me all this, but Mother still chose him. And I don't see how any of this relates to Thomas and me."

Aunt Gladys opened her lips but hesitated to speak. Something in her gaze pressed the air from Eleanore's lungs as she waited.

Finally, her aunt closed her eyes with a heavy sigh. "I'd hoped you'd never need to know this."

"What?" Eleanore took her aunt's hands and gently squeezed her wrinkled fingers. "Please, tell me."

Her aunt's piercing cornflower-blue eyes searched hers. "What do you remember of your mother's death?"

"Only that the ailment that had plagued her for years finally got the upper hand." No one had ever given her a clear answer as to which illness had taken her. It was one of the few mysteries Eleanore had never solved. She'd been but five years old when Mother passed away, too young to understand anything beyond the truth that Mother was gone and wouldn't be coming back. By the time she'd grown old enough to know what questions to ask, pressing her father or their servants for answers hadn't seemed right. And truthfully, she hadn't really wanted to know the grim details of Mother's death. They wouldn't bring her back, so what was the point?

Now, though, her aunt's words sparked a worry that Eleanore should have asked these questions sooner. "But there's more to it, isn't there?"

"I'm afraid so." Tears shimmered in her eyes. "Born to wealth and privilege, the only daughter of one of New York's most respected families, your mother was doted on by her parents and eagerly welcomed wherever she went. More than that. Families who succeeded in enticing her to their events crowed about her attendance for months. The idea of rejection, for her, was utterly inconceivable."

Realization sank like a stone in her stomach. "But marrying father changed that."

Aunt Gladys drew out her handkerchief and wiped tears from her cheeks. "Overnight, your mother went from being the princess of New York to a social leper. Those she considered her closest friends snubbed her in the street without hesitation. Her own parents disowned her, refused her admittance at their door, and returned her letters unopened. Even her elder brother refused to acknowledge her."

"But your friends and Father's friends welcomed her."

"Some did, but as I said, Rupert had been considered a great catch, and many jealous women viewed shunning your mother as her just due for stealing the prize they'd considered theirs. Even those who accepted her did so reluctantly."

"But why?"

"You have to understand, women of my social standing had been trying for years to climb higher, and families like your mother's were the primary impediment to their success. They saw no reason why they should warmly welcome your mother into their circles when her family had been shutting them out for generations." Aunt Gladys shook her head. "Your mother went from being constantly surrounded by admirers to having only a small group of near strangers willing to tolerate her presence."

Poor Mother. "But what about her illness? What does all of this have to do with that?"

"Your mother's illness was one of the mind, I'm afraid." Aunt Gladys looked toward the window with a sad smile.

Her mind? "But she was confined to her bed." Eleanore recalled the one happy memory she had of her mother. "Except for that last Christmas." She vaguely remembered being excited that Mother had finally left her room.

Aunt Gladys nodded somberly. "Through the other

eleven months of the year, coaxing your mother from her darkened chambers was an almost impossible task. Yet each December, your mother came alive. Her awakening began with overseeing the decorating of the house over the last week of November and continued through the hosting of weekly dinners. Her joy culminated with your parents' annual ball, hosted the day after Christmas. But then..."

Fragments of memory flashed in Eleanore's mind as her aunt spoke. Too young to participate, Eleanore had peeked through the second-floor railing as a seemingly endless stream of elegant women and gentlemen entered their home and disappeared into the ballroom. Once or twice, she'd managed to sneak downstairs and spy on the beautiful dancers. Mother had looked happier than Eleanore had ever seen her that night. But by noon the following day, Mother had returned to her bed and refused to leave it for days, no matter how Eleanore pleaded for her attention.

Aunt Gladys heaved a sigh. "Many men would have had their wives committed to an asylum, but not your father. No, he loved your mother despite her coldness and couldn't bear to part from her, even on her darkest days."

Eleanore considered the many days and weeks Mother had spent in her darkened room in a new light. "Then how did she...?" Her words trailed off with the memory of Father's reaction to the news about Lottie's supposed suicide. *Not again.* Eleanore caught her aunt's gaze. "Mother took her own life?"

Aunt Gladys nodded, tears spilling unchecked. "I'm afraid so."

Pain and anger warred within Eleanore. How could Mother have left her like that? Yes, Mother had lost much in marrying Father, but she'd gained a daughter. Didn't Eleanore's life count for something? Why hadn't Mother loved her enough to stay?

As if reading Eleanore's mind, Aunt Gladys took her by the shoulders with a fervent expression. "Your mother loved you, never doubt that. For years, you were the only bright spot in her life. When I visited, you were the only one who could convince her to leave her room and join us. You were the only one that brought a smile to her eyes and not just her lips."

"Then why did she choose to leave me?"

Aunt Gladys shook her head. "I can't answer that. But I am as certain that she loved you as I am that the sun will rise in the morning." She lifted her handkerchief and wiped at Eleanore's damp cheeks.

Eleanore pulled her own from her sleeve and blew her nose. Was Aunt Gladys right? Eleanore tried to imagine the isolation and grief Mother must have suffered—to make sense of Mother's choice—but she couldn't erase the sting of abandonment.

Aunt Gladys put away her handkerchief with a heavy sigh. "I hope you can see now that your father is just doing the best he knows how to protect you from your mother's fate."

Eleanore straightened. "I am not my mother. I don't need society's acceptance to be happy." Doubt drew her to study her aunt. "You wouldn't turn me away if I chose to marry Thomas, would you?"

Aunt Gladys smiled and patted Eleanore's cheek. "Of course not. You are my precious niece whom I love dearly. Nothing you do could ever change that."

Eleanore wrapped her arms around her aunt, settling her cheek against the older woman's silver hair. "I love you too."

Aunt Gladys returned the hug, then leaned back to look her in the eye. "But though I'm loath to admit it, I'm an old woman and won't be around forever. You need to seriously consider what you want the rest of your life to look like and who you want by your side as you live it. The man you marry needs to be godly, for certain. And he ought to love you. But as wonderful as a godly, loving husband is, don't discount the value of true female friendships."

Eleanore considered the small group of women she regarded as friends back in New York. If she married Thomas, would they turn their backs on her as Mother's friends had? Even if they didn't, Eleanore would be living on the opposite side of the country from them. Was that something she was willing to accept?

Aunt Gladys interrupted her thoughts before she found an answer. "And, dear, I feel that I must add, love doesn't pay the bills. I know that doesn't seem important right now, but will you be able to say the same when you're faced with choosing between paying the rent or buying new shoes for your growing son? Or when your daughter comes to you in tears because one of her playmates has a pretty new dress, while she's forced to wear patched skirts? And how much writing do you think you'll have time for without servants? Is marrying Thomas worth giving up your career?"

~

*A*s Thomas entered the bustling ballroom, his gaze swept the grand space until it caught on Clarence standing in front of the stage supervising.

All around the room, staff worked to transform the already impressive space into one filled with Christmas cheer. The large pine boughs, potted poinsettias, and gold ribbon all reminded him of Mother's fondness for the holiday season. Tears blurred the edges of his vision as a lump clogged his throat. She would have loved the changes taking place. He closed his eyes and ducked his head.

She's in Your hands now, Lord. Thank You for letting me have her as long as I did.

Thomas sucked in a breath and squeezed back tears. With his composure restored, he opened his eyes and straightened. Clarence had yet to notice him.

Thomas crossed the room to stand beside him. He

waited for Clarence to finish giving instructions to another man before addressing his friend in a hushed tone. "Clarence, I need to speak with you in private."

Clarence turned toward Thomas, brows furrowed. "Can't it wait for our afternoon fishing?" He gestured around the room. "We're rather busy here."

"No, it's about something I saw last night." Thomas gave his friend a meaningful look.

Clarence's expression flickered through surprise, then fear, and finally resignation. He told the rest of the staff to continue their work, promising to return shortly. Then he led Thomas from the room.

They strode through the courtyard to a room at the far back of the hotel. Clarence produced a key and let them in. "The suite is empty until tomorrow."

Thomas followed him inside and closed the door. "What were you doing near the powerhouse last night, Clarence? And don't lie to me this time."

Clarence turned to face him in the suite's parlor room. A glimmer of guilt crossed his features before he sighed heavily. "I'm sorry. I should have told you the truth before, but I'd promised Abigail I wouldn't—"

"Abigail Turner?" Thomas recognized the name of one of the hotel's maids.

Clarence nodded. "I suppose there's no use hiding it any longer." A bashful grin filled his face. "We've been seeing one another in secret." His expression sobered. "We've done nothing to be ashamed of, and my intentions are purely honorable. But you know the policy against staff becoming romantically involved. We can't risk being let go."

Then Thomas's suspicions had been correct. "Why not just tell me when I asked? You knew I wouldn't report you."

"Well, normally, I know you wouldn't. But after what you said the other day about love being like a match and all that...you sounded so bitter, I wasn't sure."

Conviction squeezed his heart. "I was bitter. You were right. But I've learned some things since then, and..." The memory of Eleanore's angry figure storming away froze his tongue. Had he learned? Or had his bitterness just been waiting beneath the surface for an excuse to spew forth? He mentally shoved the worry down for another time. "I'm sorry I made you wonder if you could trust me." He held out his hand. "Congratulations. I'm happy for you both. Truly."

"Thanks." Clarence accepted his hand, and they shook with silly grins on their faces. "If you want, I can tell you more when we go fishing."

"I'd like that." Thomas glanced at his watch. "Before you go, though, can you tell me anything else about Monday night?"

Clarence's cheer vanished. "You mean the night Miss Berdan suicided."

Thomas shook his head. "That's the thing. Eleanore's convinced she didn't. She thinks Miss Berdan was murdered."

Clarence jerked back. "You can't think that I—"

"No, of course not." Thomas raised a calming hand. "I'm just wondering if you remember seeing anything while you were outside."

Clarence set his hands on his hips and stared at the carpet. After a long moment, he shook his head. "I'm sorry. The only thing I remember was Abigail."

"Are you sure? You don't remember anything about that night that was different from the other nights you've met Miss Turner? Anything at all?"

"Well, it was storming, but you already knew that." Clarence scratched his jaw as he regarded the ceiling. "Abigail was unusually late in meeting me. She mentioned something about a guest demanding she deliver a note to one of the other guests, but I was so relieved to see her...I can't remember the names."

"And this occurred shortly before midnight?"

"Just after, I'd say. Abigail didn't meet me until almost twelve-thirty."

That meant there had been someone else up and about near the hour of Lottie's death. "Thank you, Clarence." Thomas patted his friend on the shoulder and turned for the door. He needed to find Eleanore.

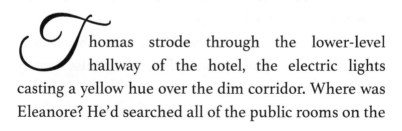

*T*homas strode through the lower-level hallway of the hotel, the electric lights casting a yellow hue over the dim corridor. Where was Eleanore? He'd searched all of the public rooms on the ground floor and even braved knocking on the door to her suite with no success. If she were any other woman, he wouldn't bother checking this lower level dominated by mostly men's rooms. But there were the ladies' lanes at the bowling alley, and he wouldn't declare much beyond Eleanore's gumption. If she thought there was a clue to be found, she'd be down here.

As he approached the men's billiards room, a familiar male voice slowed his steps until he stopped just out of sight of the room's occupants. The heavy wooden door hadn't been fully closed.

James's low voice resonated with frustration. "Of course I looked, but it wasn't there... Yes, I'm sure. Do you think I'd be careless with something like this? I know how it would look."

What was he talking about? And who was he speaking to?

Thomas couldn't make out the words of the other male in the room.

When James spoke again, his tone dripped with disdain. "I don't understand why you're so worried. I said it wasn't in her room, and it's not as though she's going to tell anyone where the jewelry came from. She's dead."

A chill ran down Thomas's spine. James could only be speaking of Lottie. Clearly, he'd lied to Eleanore, but what jewelry were they referring to? And who had let the man into the woman's room? Was James the guest

Abigail Turner had encountered the night of Lottie's death?

His mind racing with questions, Thomas debated confronting James. But Thomas was alone and had no idea who James's companion was. Obviously, someone James trusted implicitly. If James had killed before, what would stop him from killing again to cover his tracks?

Thomas inched away from the doorway. He needed to be smart about this.

CHAPTER 14

*P*rotected from the afternoon sun by the hotel's white bathhouse, Eleanore swam in the marble-lined, ocean-fed "warm plunge." The eighty-six-degree saltwater, much warmer than the morning's sixty-one-degree ocean water, enveloped her comfortingly. Steam fogged the windows, blurring the blue sky. She paused beside Aunt Gladys, who floated with her elbows resting over the side.

Across a short marble wall—in the "cold plunge"— a group of children frolicked on the floating "horses" made from barrels with carved heads attached. They laughed and splashed beneath the vigilant gazes of the many nurses sitting on the benches that lined the walls.

Eleanore grinned. "Not exactly the quiet respite we were expecting."

"No." Mirth danced in her aunt's eyes as she watched the youngsters.

A shadow near one of the windows drew Eleanore's eye. A man outside stepped close and cupped his face against the glass. *Thomas!*

His gaze found hers, and he motioned for her to come outside, then disappeared.

She glanced around, but no one else seemed to have noticed him. Aunt Gladys's amused regard remained fixed on the playing tots.

Eleanore turned away. "I'm thirsty and going to get a drink of water. Would you like some?"

Aunt Gladys laughed over the children's antics, barely sparing her a glance. "I'm fine, thank you."

Eleanore slipped from the plunge and forced herself to stroll toward the changing room where she'd left her clothing. Once inside, she redressed and left the borrowed bathing suit on the hook in the wall. The process was frustratingly tedious.

Thomas must have discovered something in regard to Lottie's death. It was the only logical reason she could think of for his seeking her out at the bathhouse. If he'd come only to spout more nonsense about Father killing Lottie, she might throw sand in his face.

She stepped from the changing room and checked that Aunt Gladys was still preoccupied with the children before making her way to the exit. Eleanore informed the attendant that she would return momentarily.

Outside, the crisp December-first breeze chilled her

wet hair, bringing goosebumps to her skin as she crossed the sand to Thomas. "What is it?"

Without preamble, he explained about seeing Clarence and a maid outside late the night before. Then he relayed what Clarence had confessed, including the strange guest who'd delayed the maid on the night of Lottie's death.

"That does sound suspicious." Eleanore faced the hotel. "Do you know where she might be working at this time of day?"

"No, but I can find out." Thomas shifted in her periphery. "But, Eleanore, I really came to warn you to stay away from James. I think he may be dangerous."

She whirled to gape at him. "What?"

"I overheard James speaking with another man in the men's billiard room just now."

She tipped her head. "And?" Thomas had better have more reason than jealousy to make such accusations.

"He was talking about something not being in a room and missing jewelry. And he told whoever he was speaking with not to worry because *she* couldn't tell anyone because *she* was dead."

Eleanore gasped. "Are you certain that's what he said?"

"I heard him clearly." Thomas's expression was grim.

She nibbled her lower lip and stared at the

incoming waves. "That does sound bad.... But you only heard half of the conversation."

"Is there anything the other man might have said that would explain the part I heard?"

She shook her head, unable to think of anything. "But I still can't imagine James as capable of murder. There must be some explanation neither of us is thinking of."

Thomas's gaze bore into hers, his eyes a darker brown than usual. "Or your feelings for him are clouding your judgment because you don't want to believe he could be behind this."

"And jealousy is clouding yours," she shot back, her tone sharper than intended. Thank goodness she hadn't mentioned the brooch. What might Thomas say if he knew of the gift? "Did you even take the time to confirm Clarence's claims about Miss Turner before rushing over here to convince me James is guilty?"

Thomas responded with a stiff jaw. "I trust Clarence. He was telling the truth."

She scoffed and flung his own words of the night before back at him. "You fell for his lies once before. How do you know he isn't lying now?"

"Clarence only lied because he was worried I wouldn't understand after—" Thomas seemed to think better of what he'd been about to say. "He was scared of getting himself and Miss Turner fired. It makes sense that he didn't confess the whole truth right away. But the parts he hid had nothing to do with Lottie. You can't say the same for what I overheard James say."

The veracity of his claim stilled her tongue.

He crossed his arms. "Have you even spoken to your father about us?"

The sudden change of subject startled her. "Of course."

"And?"

"And he confessed everything."

Thomas's arms fell. "He did?"

She couldn't meet his gaze, still unsettled by her earlier conversation with Aunt Gladys. "Yes."

Thomas's voice dripped with derision. "But he didn't apologize."

"No."

"Eleanore?" His soft plea drew her chin up. "What does this mean for us?"

"I..." She swallowed hard, tears blurring her vision. "Father still doesn't approve."

"Shouldn't who you marry be up to you?"

Did that mean he still wanted to marry her? The look in his eyes seemed to say he did. She pressed her lips together and shook her head. "It's not that simple." A tear escaped and she wiped it away.

His shoulders squared. "Seems pretty simple to me."

A passing gentleman glanced their way and paused before drawing near. "Is this man bothering you, Miss?"

She blinked away her tears and cleared her throat. "No, thank you. He...he just brought me a bit of bad news, is all." Lifting her chin, she employed the imperious expression her aunt sometimes used with impertinent strangers and addressed Thomas as the stranger would expect. "Thank you for the information. You may go."

Thomas looked between her and the stranger, clearly not ready to be done with their conversation, but after a moment, he dipped his head and strode back toward the hotel.

The stranger tipped his hat and continued on his way.

Her heart heavy, Eleanore watched Thomas's figure disappear into the hotel. Then she shuffled back to the bathhouse. She didn't want to choose between Father and Thomas. And what about James? Even if there was a plausible explanation for what Thomas had overheard—one that didn't lead to a concealed connection between James and Lottie—she struggled to imagine a happy future with a man who held her passion for writing in such disdain.

Yet Father insisted James would make a good husband. And in many ways, she agreed. James was well-mannered, considerate, and respectable—or at least, he seemed to be. If James knew of her secret work, perhaps he would reconsider his opinion of fiction.

But would that be enough? Could she give up the love she felt for Thomas to claim the acceptance, respectability, and security a marriage to James promised? And what of his faith? She'd yet to secure an answer to whether he was a Christian.

Lord, what am I going to do?

∼

*T*homas stormed through the dimly lit corridors of the hotel's lower level, praying James was still in the billiard room.

Shoving the heavy wooden door wide open, Thomas entered the silent room. At first, he thought he was too late and James had left. Then something moved behind him, and he turned.

James sat in a darkened corner, a glass of absinthe in his hand. A half-full green bottle with a French label sat on the table beside him. His bleary eyes squinted at Thomas as though he were a fly in the man's soup. "What do you want?"

Suddenly aware that he'd raced to confront a possible killer without making a plan or bringing along the backup he'd intended to before Eleanore stirred his anger, Thomas left the door open and squared off with the wealthy, powerful man. "I overheard your conversation earlier. Give me one good reason I shouldn't call for the police to arrest you for murder."

"How dare you." James slammed his glass onto the table and rose to his feet. "I should murmur you for such accusations." The sway that forced him to place a steadying hand on the wall stole the strength from his words. As did the man's use of "murmur" when Thomas was pretty sure James had intended to say "murder."

He couldn't believe it was this easy. "Then you admit it. You murdered Lottie Berdan."

James waved his arm wildly, his speech slurring. "'Course not. That crazy trollop killed herself, and everyone knows it."

Thomas ran a hand through his hair. "Then what were you discussing in here earlier? You mentioned a dead woman and jewelry."

"Oh." James plopped back into his seat. "That."

Thomas waited, but the man didn't expound. "Explain yourself."

Again, James eyed Thomas like a bug. "Go away, bellboy."

"If you want me to keep my mouth shut about what I heard, you'd better give me a good reason."

James reached for his glass and missed, then caught it on a second try. "You heard nothin'."

"Wrong. And if you don't convince me otherwise, I'm going straight to the coroner and the police."

James took a long swig of his drink. "It was just jewelry. S'all she wanted. Not even a lot. Three necklaces and a sapphire bracelet." He shrugged. "I gave more than that to—" James cast Thomas a sideways glance and changed course. "She never said anything 'bout killing herself. What's the point of the jewelry, I ask you?" James stared up at Thomas as if he had a clue what the man was blathering about. Then James blinked and rambled slowly on, his volume rising. "I knew better than to give her blackmail. Never pay a blackmailer, Father said." His voice dropped to a whisper. "They're like leeches...once they get their...their fangs into you, they never let go. Never." He jerked a nod so hard, his oiled hair fell over his eyes, and he pushed it back with his free hand. "They'll bleed you dry." James barked a humorless laugh. "Only, it was the leech who bled this time"—his bleary eyes met Thomas's—"and left me looking the fool. Worse, I might've be named for murder if the jewels hadn't poofed."

Thomas tried to wrap his mind around the man's befuddling tale. "Are you saying Lottie was blackmailing you?"

James emptied his glass and snagged the green bottle. It took two tries and a lot of spillage, but he managed to refill it. "She saw me get tossed out."

"Of where?"

"Crooked gambling house...in San Diego." James's face flushed red. "Dirty scum cheated, I'm telling you. He cheated. I had a straight flush. No one can beat a royal flush. But he claimed he won and then they kicked me out."

James clearly didn't realize he'd just named two different poker hands. Not that it mattered. The pretentious James Mitchell had just confessed to gambling—something the Wainrights undoubtedly knew nothing about. Not to mention, the man was full-gone drunk in a public room. What would Rupert think of his prized match for Eleanore if he could see and hear him now? "So Miss Berdan saw you get kicked out and...what? Demanded that you buy her jewelry?"

"Said if I didn't, she'd tell Rupert about my 'dirty little secret.'" His sneer matched the disdain in his voice.

Thomas stepped closer to the open door. "Aren't you worried I'll tell someone?"

James laughed. "The day my word doesn't hold more weight than a bellboy's...I'll..." He looked around and snagged his hat from where it hung on the corner of a nearby chair. "I'll eat my hat." He tried to twirl the accessory and succeeded only in tossing it to the floor.

Thomas decided not to mention his personal connection to the Wainrights. Rupert might not believe Thomas, but Eleanore would. He considered the sozzled man before him. "So you killed Miss Berdan to keep her from demanding more?"

"No!" Again, James rose to his feet, but this time, he fell hard against the wall. "I wanted to. But that witch" —James fumbled for something in his pocket—"wasn't worth it. Look." He produced a slip of paper that he waved in Thomas's face. "See, this receipt says I purchased the jewelry for her on Monday morning." He said the last two words in singsong, then jabbed a finger in Thomas's face. "Why would I do that if I was going to kill her?"

The man had a point. A flimsy, convoluted one. But

it was there, somewhere in the jumble of words pouring from his lips. Yet there was still the possibility that James had given Miss Berdan the jewels and when she demanded more, decided killing her was easier than buying her silence for the rest of their lives. But in James's current state, the man didn't seem capable of lying, let alone concocting such a complicated story.

James's eyes suddenly grew wide. "Wait, you're the one! You 'most caught me when I brought them to her room. You said she was taking a bath"—he swung his arm again, sloshing his drink across Thomas's shirt—"and I had to wait and wait and waaaait...and come back after dinner and everyone else was in bed. Couldn't get caught again."

It made sense—if he translated James's gibberish into coherent sentences. But was it true? Had James only given Lottie the jewels and left, or had he decided to end her hold over him permanently? Either way, Eleanore needed to know about this.

CHAPTER 15

$\mathcal{B}$y the time Thomas had changed his shirt after James's splashing incident, he was late returning to his duties and spent the rest of the day catching up. The next morning, a flood of new guests arrived in advance of a highly anticipated concert, keeping Thomas busy until the afternoon when he finally tracked down Abigail Turner in one of the guest suites.

She barely cast him a glance as she rushed toward the bed and began yanking the dirty blankets and sheets free. "What do you want, Thomas? I'm busy. The new guests in this room are expected to arrive in less than an hour."

"I won't get in your way, but I need to talk to you." Thomas helped her bundle the dirty linens and toss them into the laundry basket. "It's about your meeting with Clarence on the night of Miss Berdan's death."

Abigail froze in the middle of dusting the bureau, the feathers shaking in her grip. "Clarence told you?"

"He did, but I'd like to hear about that night from you, beginning with when you ended work for the night." As Thomas listened, Abigail confirmed Clarence's account of her delayed arrival due to an encounter with the mysterious stranger. "And you didn't recognize this man? He isn't one of the hotel's guests?"

"No. I'd never seen him before, and I haven't seen him since."

"Did you ask his name?"

"Yes, but he wouldn't give it. He just demanded to know Miss Berdan's room number. When I refused to give it, he pulled a note from his pocket and asked me to deliver it to her." Tears welled in her eyes. "I didn't think it'd do any harm, so I agreed but made sure he didn't follow me. I was in such a hurry, and the man was so creepy. I just wanted him to go away so I could meet Clarence. I never thought..." Her trembling fingers covered her lips. "You don't think whatever was in that note made her..." The maid swallowed visibly. "Do you?"

Thomas wanted to reassure her but couldn't without more information. "You didn't read the note, did you?"

"I'd never read a guest's messages." She shook her head vigorously.

"Did he say anything else?

"He asked about someplace a couple might meet in

private." Her cheeks pinked. "At first, I thought it was his sneaky way of letting me know that Clarence and I had been caught out. But when he didn't say anything more, I told him there were several parlors available for guest use and at that hour were likely all empty. He didn't like that idea and asked about the beach. I said the beach was usually empty after midnight, but that it wouldn't be pleasant with the storm coming in." The color left her face. "Wait. Do you think...do you think he was there when she...?"

A grim realization clenched Thomas's gut. Eleanore had been right. "I don't know for sure, but...it's possible he was." Thomas hated to scare the woman, but if this man returned, she needed to be on guard and alert others. "What's more, I think it's possible he pulled the trigger."

A startled cry burst from Miss Turner, her hands going to her stomach. "Then it's my fault."

"No." Thomas stepped closer. "The only one responsible for Miss Berdan's death is whoever fired that pistol. Whether it was Miss Berdan or this mysterious man, you are not responsible for her death." He caught her teary gaze and waited until she nodded her understanding. "Are you willing to tell the coroner everything you've just told me?"

She shook her head. "I'll lose my job. My family counts on me for my salary." She stepped back, her gaze sinking to the carpet. "I'm sorry. I can't."

Thomas heaved a sigh. "I understand. But I should

tell you, Miss Eleanore Wainright also knows of your meeting with Clarence."

Her head shot up. "A guest! But she'll tell Mr. Babcock."

"No. Miss Wainright is an old friend of mine who's concerned Miss Berdan's death isn't what it seems. I assure you, you can trust her." But this wasn't a secret that should be kept. Not entirely. "However, before the coroner concludes his inquest, he needs to know about the stranger who asked you about Miss Berdan that night. The timing is too coincidental."

She was shaking her head again before he'd finished speaking. "I can't—"

"I know. But what if I told the coroner—without giving your name? I could just say 'a maid' confided this to me." Thomas hesitated, but he must be honest. "He may insist on knowing who you are, but I'll try to convince him it isn't necessary unless this man proves relevant to how Miss Berdan died."

Miss Turner stared out the window for several long seconds, then nodded. "If he did have something to do with her death...my family will understand. I hope."

"Thank you. Now, just one more thing."

"Yes?"

"If you ever see this man again, do you promise to inform Clarence or myself right away?"

She clutched the duster to her chest. "Absolutely."

*E*leanore's plans to join Aunt Gladys in a late-afternoon donkey ride along the shore had swiftly been canceled upon the receipt of Thomas's note hinting at new information and asking Eleanore to meet him at the Coronado ferry dock. Thankfully, Father was away on business as usual and Aunt Gladys had accepted Eleanore's excuse of a headache.

Too bad the ruse had been for naught. Eleanore stepped out of the San Diego coroner's office, hands fisted and so angry she was surprised steam wasn't rising from her head. "Of all the arrogant, mulish—"

Thomas closed the door quickly as he joined her on the sidewalk. "Lower your voice. He might hear you."

"Good." She turned to glare at the name painted on the door, the official's dismissal of their claims still ringing in her ears. *I don't have time for an empty-headed maid's fantastical gossip, nor the ridiculous conjecture of two people with nothing better to do than play pretend investigators.*

"Come on." Thomas took her by the arm and began steering her toward the nearest streetcar. "If we don't hurry, we'll miss the next ferry."

The chilly December air bit at Eleanore's cheeks as the trolley carried them down the bustling streets of downtown San Diego. The sun was beginning its descent, casting long shadows over the cobblestone sidewalks.

"I can't say I'm surprised," Thomas murmured

beside her, a frown marring his handsome face. "As soon as the man said the jury had already submitted their conclusion of suicide based on the coroner's own inquest and that the result had been sent to the newspaper, it was clear we were wasting our time. Taking us seriously would've meant publicly admitting he'd made mistakes with his investigation."

Eleanore squeezed the purse in her hands. "You're right, but we can't just let this go."

"No, we can't," Thomas agreed as the streetcar came to a stop near the wharf. "We owe it to Lottie to find out the truth, no matter what the coroner says."

But with no idea who the creepy mystery man was and the coroner unwilling to investigate, where did they go from here?

～

Thomas led Eleanore onto the ferry, preoccupied with figuring out what to do after the coroner's mocking dismissal of their concerns. If he hadn't caught Clarence and Abigail sneaking away from the powerhouse, they'd never have known about the mystery man. Was it possible other staff had encountered this man the night of Lottie's death? Should they interview every hotel employee? He couldn't imagine Mr. Babcock being pleased with that course of action. No doubt, the hotel's manager and owners would be grateful to see the morbid ordeal put behind them.

Unexpected death wasn't exactly a selling feature for a resort billing itself as beneficial for one's health.

"What's the meaning of this?" Rupert's sharp voice cut through Thomas's musing and caused him to whirl around. Eleanore's father stormed across the deck of the ferry to stand before them. "Eleanore, what are you doing away from the hotel with this boy?"

Thomas stiffened, but before he could say a word, Eleanore replied.

"He's no longer a boy, Father. You can see very well he's a grown man."

"Even worse." Seeming to suddenly realize the attention his initial confrontation had drawn, Rupert stepped closer and practically hissed, "The two of you have no chaperone. What were you thinking?"

Eleanore squared her shoulders and glared right back at her father. "I was thinking that my sister has been murdered and Thomas and I are the only ones who seem to care about finding her killer."

Thomas couldn't allow Eleanore to take all the blame. "It was my suggestion that we visit the coroner once we discovered—"

"Of course it was your idea to wander the streets alone with my daughter. You never did have a care for her future." He turned back to Eleanore. "Did you even consider what James would think if he heard about you gallivanting with another man?"

Eleanore rolled her eyes. "We were hardly galliv—"

"I'd have thought you'd show more respect after your acceptance of his courtship."

Rupert's words were like a kick to Thomas's chest.

"What are you talking about?" Eleanore's shocked confusion was somewhat mollifying. "I never accepted—"

"Don't lie to me, Daughter. I saw the brooch box on your vanity."

"You knew about the brooch?"

"Of course. A gentleman doesn't gift something like that to an unmarried lady without first gaining approval from her father."

Thomas held a hand up. "Wait. So you did accept James's offer to court you?"

"No!" Eleanore shook her head. "James never said a thing about courtship."

Father huffed as the ferry pulled to a stop at Coronado's wharf. "Why did you think he gave you such an expensive bit of jewelry?"

Eleanore's furrowed brow did little to reassure Thomas. "He said it was a token of his friendship."

Thomas fisted his hands at his sides as passengers began streaming past them. "But you did accept his gift?"

"Yes, but—"

"There! You see?" Rupert all but crowed his victory. "Whether the words were spoken or not, accepting his gift was the same as agreeing to his courtship. Which means you have no business spending time with another man."

Rupert was right. Even he knew expensive gifts always came with strings attached. How could Eleanore have accepted jewelry from James? Hadn't she almost kissed Thomas the first night they'd met in secret? Or had that been his imagination? He'd thought after their conversation about Rupert's deception that she'd understood his absence and forgiven him. Some foolish part of him had even believed that when this whole investigation was over, she planned to choose him over James. What a fool he was.

"Now, come." Rupert took Eleanore's elbow and propelled her onto the dock. "It's clear I cannot trust you away from our rooms on your own. So until my meetings have concluded at the end of this week, that is where you will remain unless your aunt is at your side. I shall inform her of this arrangement as soon as we return."

Eleanore dug her heels into the wood of the wharf. "Father! I am not a child—"

"Precisely why you need a chaperone." He continued to tug Eleanore along the dock toward the station, leaving Thomas no choice but to trail behind. "I will also make it clear to Gladys that Thomas Harding is to keep his distance from you from now on."

Eleanore stepped aboard the train and plopped onto a bench beside an open window. "Father, that isn't your decision to make." The fire in her words sparked hope in Thomas that perhaps she did still care for him.

Rupert sat beside his daughter. "It is, if he wants to keep his job."

About to board, Thomas froze at the hard look in the man's gaze.

"If you come anywhere near my daughter again, I'll personally ensure you no longer have a job at the Hotel del Coronado or any other reputable hotel in the country."

The bell rang, alerting passengers that the train was about to depart.

Sick to his stomach, Thomas stepped away from the car and watched it pull out. He'd taken a job as a bellboy at the Hotel del Coronado so he could study what it took to run something like a sanitarium. More than that, he'd hoped to work his way into higher positions while gaining experience and connections that might someday enable him to realize his dream of opening a health resort for all classes. If Rupert Wainright used his influence against Thomas, he wouldn't just lose his job. He'd lose his chance at his dream. He couldn't risk that for a woman who didn't seem to want him. No matter how much his heart yearned for her.

CHAPTER 16

*E*leanore spun from the door Father had just slammed shut behind him to address her aunt. "Why does he refuse to listen to reason?" She flung herself onto her bed, glaring at the ceiling. "Doesn't he even care how I feel about things?"

Her aunt came to sit beside her. "Of course he does. He's your father. He'll always love you."

"Then why won't he let me choose who I want for a husband? Doesn't he want me to be happy?"

"Eleanore, stop being dramatic. You know your father wants your happiness. It's just that he isn't convinced you're mature enough to know how to achieve that in the long term."

"Well, how am I supposed to convince him if he dismisses everything I say?"

"For one thing, you can sit up and stop whining like a child."

Aunt Gladys's unexpectedly stern tone shocked the fury from her system. She sat up. "I'm sorry. You're right. He's just so..." Lacking the words, she released a growl.

Her aunt chuckled. "You should have known him as a teenager. Oh my." Her gaze grew distant for a moment before she blinked and turned back to Eleanore. "But in any case, letting your frustration get the best of you is no way to prove you're ready to make your own life decisions."

Eleanore took a long, deep breath. "All right. I'm calm. Now, what do I do? How can I convince Father that marrying Thomas is what will make me truly happy, not just now, but until I am old and gray?"

Aunt Gladys patted her silvery hair and pointedly cleared her throat.

Eleanore's cheeks warmed, and she wrapped an arm around her aunt. "You know I didn't mean anything unkind."

Aunt Gladys released her mock stern expression with a smile. "Yes, I do. Now, as for your trouble, I think the thing that will most convince your father is for you to simply decide."

Eleanore stared at her aunt. "But I have decided. I want—"

"Have you?" Aunt Gladys's keen eyes made Eleanore squirm. "Because it seems to me a young woman intent on marrying one man would have told said man of her heart and wouldn't be accepting jewelry from any other man who wasn't her relative."

Why hadn't she told Thomas that she loved him? Eleanore's shoulders sagged. If she was completely honest with herself, she'd known deep down that the brooch meant more than just friendship to James. It was why she'd determined to return it. But Aunt Gladys was right. She'd kept her feelings from Thomas and accepted the gift from James because a part of her was still torn between the two possible futures, despite her questions about James's faith and confidence in Thomas's.

Before the revelation of James's drunken confession, a small voice had warned her against shutting the door on a future as Mrs. James Mitchell. Even now, that quiet voice argued that marriage to a wealthy man would ensure she could continue her writing, at least in secret. But marriage to Thomas—a man unlikely to ever garner enough income to hire a household of servants —would probably mean an end to the free time and energy she needed to create her novels. Her writing wasn't just a hobby. The stories she wrote were a part of her heart poured onto the page.

Was marriage to Thomas worth giving up part of who she was?

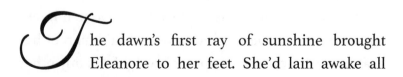

The dawn's first ray of sunshine brought Eleanore to her feet. She'd lain awake all night, debating the wisdom of defying Father—of risking her private passion for a life spent with Thomas —and had finally found her answer. She only prayed that Thomas still felt the same after Father's words yesterday.

As she dressed for the day, Eleanore prayed that Aunt Gladys's belief in Father's compassion would prove true. As much as Eleanore wanted to live her life alongside the man she loved and was willing to place her own pursuits in question to make that happen, she couldn't bear the thought of costing Thomas his dream of owning a sanitarium.

Ready to face Father, Eleanore paused beside her aunt's bed.

Silver hair streaming across her pillow, the older woman grinned up at her. "Nervous?"

Eleanore nodded. "Will you pray with me?"

"Of course."

They joined hands, and Eleanore poured her heart out to the One who truly held her future in His hands.

~

*M*ind racing, Thomas disembarked the train and sped toward the hotel. He'd been awake all night considering Rupert's threats and Eleanore's decision to accept James's jewelry. Though he'd initially agreed with Rupert that the gift meant more than friendship, if that was all it meant to Eleanore, Thomas owed it to her to fight for their love. Because no matter what Rupert or James believed, Eleanore could be happy as Thomas's wife. At least he knew he'd do everything in his power to make it so.

More importantly, just as dawn turned the black of night to gray, Thomas had remembered that Rupert Wainright wasn't in control of anyone's future. That power belonged to God alone. So long as Thomas continued to seek God's guidance, comfort, and strength, he could face whatever his future held.

He reached the ramp that descended to the employee entrance near the back of the hotel, and his steps stuttered. Nearly the entire width of the passageway was blocked by trunks, bags, and crates stacked as tall as Thomas. Had a circus arrived?

Clarence emerged from the melee and rushed to meet Thomas. "Thank goodness you're early. Romandy's Hungarian Orchestra is finally here, and we've four men out sick. I need your help."

Thomas opened his mouth to protest, but Clarence grabbed his arm and dragged him toward the nearest pile. His friend pointed at various luggage, spouting off room numbers so fast Thomas scrambled to memorize them all. Then Clarence disappeared back down the ramp, already shouting orders at another employee.

Resisting the urge to kick the stack of trunks and carpet bags, Thomas set to work. His conversation with Eleanore would have to wait.

Duty kept Thomas running to and fro until his afternoon break. The moment he was released, Thomas made his way to Eleanore's room, praying she'd be inside. He hadn't encountered her on any of his many morning tasks.

He reached her door, took a deep breath, and knocked firmly. The cost of defying Rupert would be steep, but he couldn't let fear dictate his choices any longer.

Lord, be with me. Guide my words and actions.

Gladys Wainright answered the door, her expression unreadable. "I'm sorry, Mr. Harding, but Eleanore is not receiving visitors."

Thomas tried to peer past the woman's shoulder. Was Eleanore listening? "Please, Miss Wainright, I must speak with her. I need to tell her how much I love her and that I'm not afraid of her father's threats. Not anymore."

Eleanore's soft voice rose from somewhere in the room. "Do let him in, Aunt, please."

"One moment." Miss Wainright stepped back and closed the door, leaving just a crack open.

Unable to resist, Thomas leaned his ear toward the opening.

Miss Wainright's hushed voice spoke first. "I thought we'd agreed that you needed to speak with your father before speaking with Mr. Harding."

Thomas's chest expanded. Eleanore wanted to speak with him. Surely, that was a good sign.

"We did, and I tried. But that was before Father refused to hear me and left without word of when he'd return. We've been waiting for hours."

"I still think it best to make things right with your father first."

"Please, Aunt. I must speak with Thomas. I need to know how he feels."

Unable to wait a moment longer, Thomas pushed the door open and crossed the room to where Eleanore sat. He dropped to his knee and took her hands in his. "Eleanore, I love you, and I want to spend my life with you, if you'll have me. Please say you will."

Eleanore's eyes glistened over a bright smile. "I love you, too, Thomas, and I would be honored to call you my husband."

Thomas squeezed her hands, wanting nothing more than to take her into his arms and claim her lips, but he held back. He needed to know. "What about your father?"

Her expression sobered. "I can't promise he won't have you fired or cause problems for us if we marry."

He shook his head. "That's not what I meant." He cupped her face in one hand. "I know you love him and his blessing is important to you."

She nodded, a tear escaping each eye. "It is, and I pray he will give his blessing once he understands that nothing else in this life, apart from God, can make me as happy as being your wife."

"And if he doesn't?"

Eleanore leaned forward, taking his face in hers. "Then we'll cross that bridge together." She stole any response he might have made by placing her lips on his in a kiss that revealed how true and strong her love for him was.

CHAPTER 17

*H*and in hand with Thomas, Eleanore waited beside her aunt as the elevator lowered them to the first floor. Thomas's request to confront Father in a more neutral location rather than the Wainrights' guest suite made complete sense to her. Father was far more likely to control his temper if there was a chance of being overheard. She only hoped with the many new guests who'd arrived yesterday there would still be a parlor available for reservation. They would require some semblance of privacy.

Once the elevator stopped and the attendant opened its golden gates, Thomas waved for Aunt Gladys to precede them into the rotunda. As anticipated, a fire burned in the large fireplace, and the lobby was crowded with men discussing their day's catch while waiting for the hotel's chef to collect that which would be added to the evening's meal. The chatter of women's voices drifted down from the second-story balcony, where many observed their husbands, brothers, or fathers from above. One couple, seemingly newly arrived, followed a porter carrying their luggage toward the elevator. Another pair wandered the hall that led to the enclosed veranda.

A young maid passed the latter couple and began crossing to the stairs beside the elevator. Her gaze flicked toward the front desk. She stopped midstride, her face turning splotchy as she stared at a man speaking with the front desk clerk. Then she whirled and nearly collided with Eleanore and Thomas.

Thomas caught the maid's shoulder with his free hand. "Whoa, Abigail. Is everything all right?"

For a moment, Eleanore stiffened at Thomas's use of the pretty woman's Christian name. Then she recalled that Abigail Turner was the maid Clarence Blackwood was secretly wooing. The one who'd been bothered by the creepy guest who'd demanded to see Lottie. The man! Eleanore's gaze shot to the brown-haired stranger at the counter. She addressed Miss Turner without taking her eyes from the man leaning toward the front desk clerk with an intense expression, his mouth moving but voice too quiet for her to hear. "That's him, isn't it? The man who was asking about Lottie."

In her periphery, Eleanore caught Miss Turner's nod.

"We should send for the police," Thomas whispered.

"He might be gone before they arrive." Eleanore released Thomas's hand and marched across the room.

As she drew near, the man's words became clear. "I already told you. My name is Dr. Malcolm Berdan, Lottie's brother, and I demand that you release her belongings to me at once."

Had the investigator finally found Lottie's brother and sent him here? Surely not. The investigator would have contacted Eleanore for the rest of his payment, if that were the case. Either way, the man's services were no longer needed. If the angry man at the counter was who he claimed, Lottie's brother was here.

Though the clerk's response was low, it was no less firm. "And I've told you, I have no such belongings. Everything belonging to Miss Berdan was taken by the deputy coroner."

Dr. Berdan's face mottled. "Liar. I've already been to the coroner and the undertaker's, and the document isn't there. It must be here. Why do you persist in this deceit?"

Eleanore stopped beside Lottie's brother. "So that's why you demanded to speak with Lottie the night she died? You wanted a document she had?"

The man glared at her. "Who're you?"

Thomas came to her side, his eyes fixed on Dr. Berdan. "Answer the question."

"I've no idea what she's talking about since I've just arrived in Coronado this very hour." He produced a ferry ticket from his pocket. "Here's proof, should you require it."

Eleanore shook her head. "You easily could have come and gone since that night. That ticket proves nothing. We have a witness willing to testify that you were in this hotel the night of Lottie's death, demanding to know her room number. And when you could not achieve that, you insisted on a note being delivered to her room and asked about private places to meet with her."

Her confident words had drawn the attention of everyone in the room. The men's conversations and even the women's chattering from above faded to silence.

Dr. Berdan glanced nervously around before puffing his chest. "How dare you invent fantastical accusations to besmirch my character, when I've come here as a grieving brother in search of what little is left of his dear sister's life."

Eleanore opened her mouth to respond, but Thomas beat her to it. "Miss Wainright hasn't invented a thing. As she said, we have a witness."

"Not possible." The man's dark gaze slid past them, sweeping the lobby until it landed on Miss Turner and narrowed. Then he turned back to Eleanore and Thomas. "You can't possibly believe the gossip of a maid. Everyone knows servants have nothing better to do than concoct entertaining gossip for the sole purpose of breaking up the monotony of their dreary lives."

"Aha!" Eleanore jabbed her own finger into the condescending man's chest. "And how did you know who our witness was?"

Eyes wide, Miss Turner wilted into herself and began shuffling backward until Aunt Gladys's arm came around her.

Dr. Berdan stepped away. "Because you said...you—" He spun and dashed for the door, but two male employees blocked the door while another two grabbed the doctor's arms and wrestled him to the ground.

"What are you doing? Unhand me." The doctor fought his captors to no avail. "You have no reason to detain me. Even if I was here that night, Lottie killed herself. The papers said so."

Eleanore crossed to stand over him. "The papers are wrong." Something shiny peeked from the doctor's coat pocket. Was that...? Eleanore swooped down and dug her fingers into the pocket. When she drew back, three necklaces and a bracelet dangled from her fist.

"Thief! Those are mine!" James stormed across the room. "Give them to me." He held his hand out for the jewels, but she pulled her hand back, knowing—thanks to Thomas—that there was more to the story.

The doctor scowled as he continued squirming against the restraining grips of the men holding him. "You're wrong. They're mine. I bought them for...my wife."

Thomas glared down at him. "It took you a moment too long to come up with that lie." He turned toward James. "Do you still have that receipt?"

James immediately withdrew a slip of paper from his pocket and held it up for the room to see. "This is a receipt proving that jewelry belongs to me. This man is a thief."

Thomas grimaced. "That's not entirely accurate."

James narrowed his eyes at Thomas in clear warning.

Thomas ignored him and addressed their fascinated audience of hotel guests and employees. "Yesterday afternoon, Mr. Mitchell confessed to me that he'd purchased these jewels for Miss Berdan and had given them to her prior to her death. And I was present during the inspection of both Miss Berdan's person and her room." He turned back to the doctor. "These jewels were not found. And James didn't give them to her until long after supper Monday night. Which means you must have taken them from her and were the last one to see her alive. Maybe even the one responsible for her death."

Panic flared in Dr. Berdan's eyes, though his expression remained defiant. "You're crazy. I would never—"

"No, he's right." Eleanore's mind whirled, putting all the pieces together, and landed on the article about a Dr. Fielding that she'd found under Lottie's mattress. "And I think I know why you did it, Dr. Fielding."

The man's defiance melted into shock. "How—"

"You've been blackmailing Lottie, threatening to reveal her medical condition to the world, just as you did to your patients in Chicago. But when she refused to pay for your silence, you killed her."

Dr. Fielding burst into hysterical laughter. "Me, blackmail her? If only I'd been clever enough. No, my little half sister was always the clever one. If only I'd realized how devious she was sooner. I might have spared the patients whose files she stole from my office the humiliation of having their private conditions exposed and myself from two years in prison for a crime my sister committed. Not to mention the loss of everything I'd done to scrape and claw my way out of the gutter our mother left us in."

Confusion muddied Eleanore's thoughts. "What are you talking about? You're the criminal—the one sick enough to kill his own sister."

"'Sick.'" Again the man laughed with no humor. "That's what she was supposed to be. The arsenic I've been adding to her morning coffee since I was released from prison should have killed her long before she made it to this wretched hotel. But I was weak. Too scared of being caught. Then she found out and ran."

Eleanore swallowed against the bile rising up her throat. She'd done enough research for her novels to know that large amounts of arsenic could quietly kill a person. No wonder Lottie had appeared so ill. "How could you poison an innocent woman?"

Dr. Fielding's face turned a dark red. "Aren't you

listening? Lottie was evil from the day she was born. She never knew a moment of remorse."

True or not, it was clear the man before her believed what he was saying. "So you followed her here and killed her."

"She left me no choice!" With a sudden lunge, he broke free of the men holding him and sprinted outside.

Thomas and Eleanore gave chase along with most of the onlookers.

Thomas reached the man first, tackling him at the bottom of the stairs. They wrestled in a tangle of limbs on the drive until more men joined in, securing the doctor once more.

Thomas stood, breathing heavily and his lip bleeding. "Check his pockets. He was reaching for something."

Seeming exhausted and defeated, Dr. Fielding lay still as two men picked his pockets and discovered a pistol that looked the same as the one Eleanore had seen beside Lottie's body.

"You should be thanking me." The trapped man raged at those around him. "She was more of a poison to this world than the arsenic I gave her. If I hadn't stopped her, she'd only have continued ruining the lives of everyone she met." His furious eyes met hers. "You of all people should understand why I had to do it."

Eleanore gasped. He knew of her connection to Lottie?

"She's been bleeding your father dry from the day she discovered who he was, and she'd never have stopped."

Eleanore fisted her hands, her eyes stinging with unshed tears. "She was my sister! And no matter what she may or may not have done, you had no right to take her life." Thanks to him, Eleanore would never get a chance to truly know her only sibling. The thought weakened her knees, but Thomas's comforting arm came around her waist, steadying her.

Someone must have summoned the police because they suddenly appeared and took custody of Dr. Fielding. They also took the jewels Eleanore had been holding the entire time.

"Hey!" James protested. "Those belong to me." He tried to show them his receipt, but they took the paper and informed him the jewelry was now considered evidence in a crime and he'd have to make his case to a judge if he wanted them back.

The police began leading Dr. Fielding away, James on their heels, still arguing. Beyond them, the train pulled to a stop near the end of the drive and Father disembarked. His gaze roamed from the departing policemen to James before moving farther up the drive and spotting Eleanore with Thomas's arm still around her waist.

CHAPTER 18

Thomas kept his arm tight around Eleanore's waist as Rupert Wainright strode up the drive toward them. Still gossiping about the scandalous events, most of those who'd been drawn into the scene that had just unfolded returned inside, seemingly unaware of the wealthy magnate's furious approach.

As soon as the man was within speaking distance, he spat out, "Get your arm off my daughter."

Thomas started to loosen his grip, but Eleanore clasped his fingers, keeping him in place.

"No, I want him here." He felt her take a deep breath. "There's a lot we need to speak with you about."

"Nonsense. You're obviously overwrought by whatever that was." He gestured back to where the policemen were loading Dr. Fielding onto a wagon. "And you aren't thinking clearly." He faced the hotel's manager who hadn't yet returned inside. "Mr. Babcock,

I must insist you fire this man immediately for his impertinent behavior toward my daughter."

This wasn't how this was supposed to go. Thomas had known losing his position was a possibility, but he'd hoped for at least a few minutes alone to convince Rupert not to follow through on his threats. Thomas pulled away, and this time, Eleanore let him go.

She moved to stand beside her father and addressed Thomas's employer, her voice clear and unwavering. "You can't fire him. He's done nothing wrong."

While he deeply appreciated her defense of him, Thomas could speak for himself. He opened his mouth to do just that, but Mr. Babcock spoke first.

"She's right," he told Rupert. "Your daughter has just endured a rather upsetting scene, and from my view, Mr. Harding was providing needed support and comfort. What's more, she clearly stated that his assistance was welcome."

Rupert blustered, "She's young. She doesn't know what she wants. And if you don't fire him, I'll be sure to inform every man I know that the Hotel del Coronado refuses to protect its unmarried female guests."

Mr. Babcock held up a hand. "Please cease causing a scene, Mr. Wainright. We've had quite enough of that today. While I am grateful that you've chosen to spend your winter season here at the Hotel del Coronado and would appreciate your recommendation among your acquaintances, I'm not about to fire the man who just assisted in the arrest of a murderer." Mr. Babcock smiled reassuringly at Thomas as he continued. "Mr. Harding has a sterling reputation here at the hotel for being honest, kind, generous, respectful, and responsible. Exactly the type of employee that exemplifies the quality our hotel stands for."

Thomas's heart swelled with each compliment. He'd had no idea Mr. Babcock thought so highly of him.

The hotel manager turned toward the stairs. "Now, if you'll excuse me, I have a lobby full of guests requiring reassurance." Without waiting for Rupert's reply, Thomas's employer ascended the staircase and entered the hotel.

Rupert turned back to face Eleanore and Thomas, his expression stunned. "Well, I..." He blinked and his focus fixed on his daughter. "Eleanore, please, you must reconsider. You don't know what it is to live without. Just like your mother. She didn't—"

"I'm not my mother." Eleanore stepped closer to Thomas's side and slipped her arm through his. "I know what I want—who I want—and what I'm willing to sacrifice to keep him by my side." She reached her free hand toward her father, pleadingly. "Please, don't make me choose between you. Our story doesn't need to be the same as it was between Mother and her parents." Her warm gaze moved from Rupert to Thomas's and back again. "I want you both in my life."

Thomas finally found a moment to speak. "Sir, I love your daughter more than anything else in this world, and I promise to do everything I can to make her happy. But I know that desire will be far easier to achieve with you in her life."

Rupert's mouth parted, but Thomas wasn't finished.

"Not because of your money, but because you're her father and she loves you." Thomas draped his arm across Eleanore's shoulders and drew her against his side. She wrapped her arm around his waist. "We'd both like you to be part of our lives." He prayed the subtle message that he planned to marry Eleanore with or without Rupert's blessing wouldn't stir the man's pride into refusing to give it.

Gladys Wainright moved to Eleanore's other side. "Don't be a fool, Rupert," she said, her tone stern.

Mr. Wainright gaped at his older sister. "You approve of this?"

"I do." She smiled. "Mr. Harding has proven himself to be an upright, courageous young man who loves our girl more than his own wants and desires. You warned him he'd lose everything by pursuing her, but he's still here fighting for her. Don't you want Eleanore to have a husband who'll love and support her, putting her hopes and desires before his own?"

Rupert's mouth closed, and he looked between them for a long moment before fixing his gaze on Eleanore. "You're sure this is what you want?"

She gave Thomas a squeeze. "I'm sure."

Rupert nodded and stuck out his hand. "Then I give you permission to court my daughter."

Relief and joy coursed through Thomas as he accepted the man's shake. "Tha—"

"On one condition." The man's grip tightened as his narrowed look speared Thomas.

"Father!"

Rupert ignored his daughter's gasp of protest and waited for Thomas's response.

"What's that?"

"The two of you don't rush into marriage. Take your time. It's been two years since the you last saw one another, and at the time, you were barely on the cusp of adulthood. Get to know each other again as adults. Discuss your future. Make sure you're both certain of your plans before you make a lifelong commitment."

Though he was loath to delay claiming Eleanore as his wife, Thomas saw the wisdom in her father's words and respected them. He glanced at Eleanore, who nodded. Then he turned back to Rupert. "Agreed."

CHAPTER 19

DECEMBER 26, 1893
HOTEL DEL CORONADO

Illuminated by the steady glow of pendant lights hanging from the third-story promenade that encircled the ballroom, Eleanore laughed as Father danced her across the crowded room in time with the orchestra's lively music. The hotel's annual Christmas ball was as well-attended this year as it had been last year. The jolly guests crowding the edges of the dance floor and the charming Christmas decor that still adorned the elegant space below the vast, conical roof were little more than a blur as she stared at Father's joyous face. Who knew he had so much energy and cheer hidden beneath his usually somber facade?

He'd been gone more than present during the year that had passed since he'd given his permission for

Thomas's courtship. With Father's duties requiring his return to New York last spring, James no longer a figure in her life, and Thomas working extra hours to set money aside for their future, Eleanore had completed her latest manuscript in record time. Her publisher had been so pleased with the results, he'd requested another novel from her to be submitted next spring. With Thomas's encouragement added to Aunt Gladys's, Eleanore had found the courage to share her secret career with Father. He'd been less than pleased but had agreed not to interfere so long as she kept her pseudonym and remained unidentified as the true author behind the stories—a compromise Eleanore willingly accepted.

Beneath Aunt Gladys's watchful eye, the love Eleanore and Thomas shared had grown stronger than ever. She couldn't remember ever being so happy. Still, Father's return three weeks ago had stirred her impatience for Thomas's proposal.

He'd been acting strangely for days now, convincing Eleanore that he'd received the official blessing from Father and was planning a special moment to ask her. Christmas dinner had seemed a likely choice, yet their holiday feast had come and gone without an engagement. It was a shame he'd been required to assist below stairs this evening and wasn't able to join them, or he might have taken advantage of this last bit of Christmas celebration to ask the question.

The spirited gallop dance came to a close, and

Father led her from the dance floor into the crowd. Perhaps this wasn't the best place for Thomas to propose, after all. There wasn't room enough for him to kneel, and the enthusiastic conversations around them would make it difficult to discern his words.

Rather than stopping beside Aunt Gladys, Father kept Eleanore's hand and guided her from the ballroom. Aunt Gladys followed them into the less crowded hallway.

Hand still in Father's, Eleanore asked, "Where are we going?"

"I need some fresh air. Don't you?" Father didn't slow as he continued through the enclosed veranda and down the exterior stairs.

She took a deep breath. The brisk night air was refreshing after the body-warmed ballroom. Father didn't stop on the wide sidewalk but descended the terraced steps to the beach. With her attention focused on not tripping over the ruffled hem of her silk ballgown, it wasn't until they reached the sand that Eleanore looked toward the shore and gasped. "Thomas!"

Several feet ahead, on a patch of sand that had been raked smooth, stood Thomas. He wore a fine tuxedo and a nervous smile. Around him were placed at least a dozen gas lanterns in the shape of a heart.

Father finally stopped and released her hand. Grinning as though he'd just bought a new railroad line, he nodded toward Thomas. "Go on. Don't leave the boy waiting."

Aunt Gladys stepped up to slide her arm through Father's, her smile belying the tears in her eyes.

Eleanore narrowed her eyes. "You knew."

Aunt Gladys chuckled. "Of course I knew. Now go." She waved at Eleanore in a shooing motion.

Heart pounding, Eleanore turned back toward Thomas and slowly crossed to stand before him. Uncertain what was expected of her, she mumbled, "Hello."

Thomas's expression sobered as he took her hands in his. "Eleanore, you brought joy, companionship, and adventure to my childhood. Three years ago, I knew I wanted to keep all of those things in my life—to keep *you* in my life. The separation and pain we endured couldn't smother the flame in my heart that has always burned for you. This past year of getting to know you again has only strengthened and fed that fire. Your creativity, kindness, loyalty, courage, and faith all help to make me a better man. You help me see the world in ways I couldn't imagine without you. But no matter how I look at things, I can't imagine my future without you, and I don't want to."

Tears blurred her eyes as Thomas lowered to one knee.

"I can't promise you the kind of life you've known thus far, but I can promise that I will always love you, and that I will do everything within my power to support your dreams and make you happy."

From his pocket, Thomas pulled a gold ring featuring a large emerald surrounded by tiny diamonds. It was breathtaking. How had he afforded the purchase?

"Eleanore Kathryn Wainright, will you do me the immense honor of becoming my wife?"

"Yes!" She nodded so hard her knotted bun shook at the back of her head. "Oh, Thomas. I love you so much!"

With a grin, he tugged the glove from her hand, stuffed it into his pocket, and slid the ring onto the third finger of her left hand. Then he stood. "I—"

Unable to wait another moment, Eleanore pressed her lips to his in a kiss that she hoped expressed all the love she felt for this man, because—though words were her forte—nothing she could say seemed like enough.

A loud cheer rose up behind her, and Thomas pulled back, his cheeks adorably pink.

She turned to discover that a large portion of the night's revelers had drifted out to the walkway and witnessed their engagement. "Oh my." Engagement. Her gaze moved from the merry onlookers to the ring on her finger. She was finally engaged to Thomas! Wait. Was it her imagination, or had she seen this ring before?

Thomas held her right hand in his as Father and Aunt Gladys joined them in the heart-shaped ring of light.

Father offered his hand to Thomas. "Well done, young man. Well done."

Aunt Gladys gestured to the ring. "Do you like it?"

Eleanore grinned at Thomas. "It's beautiful." Then a memory slid into place, and she faced her aunt. "Wait. It's your ring, isn't it?"

Aunt Gladys clasped her hands over her chest, joy exuding from her very being. "It was my mother's first. She gave it to me when it became clear matrimony wasn't in my future, but now I'm thrilled for you to have it." She nodded toward Thomas. "When he mentioned that he was saving for an emerald that would match the green flecks in your eyes, I knew the ring was meant to be yours."

Eleanore released Thomas's hand to embrace her aunt, gratitude swelling her chest. "Thank you!"

"Now." Father pulled a thick envelope from his pocket and held it out to Thomas. "Consider this the first part of your wedding present."

Thomas opened the envelope, withdrew a stack of folded papers, and scanned the first document. He raised wide eyes toward Father. "This is the deed to the land I've been hoping to purchase for my sanitarium."

Father nodded. "If you read the rest of the papers, you'll see that majority ownership transfers to your name the day you wed Eleanore."

Eleanore gasped and clasped Thomas's free hand in both of hers, but Father wasn't finished.

"You'll also find an offer of investment. We can

discuss the terms later, but if you're agreeable, I'd like to join in your venture."

Thomas shifted his feet. "Sir, this is incredibly generous, but I want to be clear. The sanitarium I create will be open to people of all means."

Father waved his hand dismissively. "Yes, I'm well aware. Eleanore has written me many letters outlining what it is you hope to accomplish, and I think it's a wonderful goal. But you do need to be realistic about the expenses involved with running something like this. Which is why I've come up with a way that I think will both earn us a profit and keep the sanitarium's services available to whomever needs them."

Thomas gaped at Father for a moment. "I don't know what to say."

Father's expression turned stern. "As I said, we can negotiate the details later, but there is one thing I won't compromise on."

Thomas straightened. "And that is?"

A sparkle in Father's eye let Eleanore breathe as he replied, "The institution is to be named after your mother."

Thomas's mouth fell open, and Eleanore launched herself into Father's arms. "Thank you," she whispered.

He patted her back before drawing away to meet her gaze. "Thank you, Daughter, for showing me that some loves can withstand the fires of life without turning to ash. And for forgiving me for not understanding that sooner."

She squeezed him tighter. "I love you."

"Yes, well." Father cleared his throat and stepped back, then offered his arm to his sister. "Gladys, why don't you and I take a stroll?"

Aunt Gladys hesitated. "Weren't you planning to speak with Mr. Radmor about selling your mill?"

"Radmor will be here tomorrow." He studied the blanket of stars overhead. "Not every December night will be as fine. Come, let's enjoy it while we can."

Aunt Gladys slid her arm through Father's, and they strolled off along the shore.

Eleanore glanced at the still-burning lamps around them. "What do we do about these?"

In answer, Thomas waved toward the few lingering guests outside the hotel, and a figure separated from them. A moment later, Eleanore recognized Clarence.

"Congratulations." His wide grin included Eleanore in the sentiment as he clasped Thomas's hand and pumped it up and down. Then he gestured at the lamps. "I'll take care of these."

As Clarence began trimming the lights, Thomas offered Eleanore his arm. "Where would you like to go?"

She placed her hand on his arm and beamed up at him. "I'll be happy anywhere we go, so long as I'm with you."

ACKNOWLEDGMENTS

This book is especially rich in historical detail thanks to the tireless efforts of the Hotel del Coronado's history staff and volunteer docents who have labored for decades to preserve the unique history of this beautiful resort. My particular thanks go to Gina Petrone, Robin Siara, and Donna Robillard, who each gave of their time and knowledge to help me fill the gaps I needed for this story. Please note that I have taken some artistic liberties in writing this novel, and any mistakes are entirely my own.

I am incredibly grateful for the polishing efforts of my wonderful editor, Barbara Curtis, and the support of my publisher, Wild Heart Books.

As always, many thanks are owed to my husband and beloved children for supporting and encouraging me. And, of course, I would have no stories to tell without my loving Lord and Savior, Jesus Christ.

AUTHOR'S NOTE

Thank you for reading *A Christmas at Hotel del Coronado*. If you enjoyed this story and/or God used it to touch your heart in some way, I would love to hear from you! You can always reach me on social media or via email at WriteKathleenDenly@gmail.com. It would also really help me if you'd share your review in some way—online or off. If you'd like to keep up with my writing journey and be the first to know when my next book releases, I encourage you to join my Kathleen's Readers' Club via the form on my website: www.Kathleen-Denly.com

Many of my readers want to know which parts of my story were true to history and which were fictional. If that's you, keep reading. (P.S. There's an Easter egg in this story which I explain at the end!)

Lottie Berdan was inspired by the true historical figure Lottie Bernard, aka Kate Morgan. Although great effort has been invested by multiple people over the years to document the facts surrounding this mysterious woman's life and tragic end, there remain many unanswered questions, largely due to the era in which her death occurred. I honestly included far too many factual details in this story to list them all here, but I will highlight several that I kept and mention the significant deviations which I chose to make.

First of all, the date of Lottie's arrival at the hotel, her visits to San Diego, her strange requests of the staff, the timing and circumstances of her body's discovery, and the details of the coroner's inquest are all accurate to the best of my knowledge, with two exceptions. First, it was a hotel gardener (not a bellboy) who encountered the electrician that discovered the body, helped to cover it, and stood guard until the deputy coroner's arrival. Second, to give my entirely fictional investigators a bit more time to work through the clues of the mystery, I delayed the coroner's inquest by two days. (Think of the coroner's inquest as similar to a trial where witnesses testify regarding the facts leading up to her death and immediately following the discovery of her body, along with a presentation of evidence.) In reality, the inquest was held and concluded the day after Lottie's body was found. The results of the inquest were published the day after that.

Mr. Babcock is the real name of the hotel's manager (and co-founder), but his actions in this story are entirely fictional. For that matter, the personality of all my characters, their motives, and (most of) their actions are purely fictional—with one exception. My fictional Lottie's actions are a mix of true and fictional. Although the real Lottie did profess to having a physician brother who had her luggage claim tickets and was supposed to meet her at the hotel, that brother never showed up (in fact, we are still uncertain whether he was a fabrication), and he was certainly never charged with murder. The real Lottie also purchased a gun and had its use demonstrated to her, claiming it was a gift. However, she did so at a gun shop in San Diego and not a general store, but I needed a reason for Eleanore to witness the purchase, and some general stores did sell guns. The overheard conversation between the two men in the store was part of the testimony from the coroner's inquest.

The real Lottie also requested a bath in her room, burned papers in her fireplace, and told the chief clerk to telegram a mystery contact in Iowa (not New York) for funds to cover her stay. Everything my fictional deputy coroner found was historically accurate minus the clue pointing to Dr. Fielding.

These days, Lottie Bernard is known as Kate Morgan, the mysterious "beautiful stranger" who committed suicide on the hotel's oceanfront steps and now supposedly haunts the hotel.

If you'd like to know all the true facts regarding Lottie/Kate's life as we know them, I highly recommend the book *Beautiful Stranger: The Ghost of Kate Morgan and the Hotel del Coronado.* If you'd like to know more about the construction and incredible history of this unique resort, I recommend *Hotel del Coronado History*, *"The Loveliest Hotel You Can Imagine"* and *Building the Dream: The Design and Construction of the Hotel del Coronado.* The first two books are available through the hotel's bookstore. The last is out of print but a wonderful book if you can find a copy.

You can also find dozens of news articles printed about Lottie in the archives of newspapers published during the weeks following her death. Much like certain tragedies of our time, something about the beautiful mystery woman whose life was cut short captured our nation's attention, so accounts regarding who she was and what happened to her were written and republished in nearly every major newspaper throughout the country.

To the best of my knowledge, the setting, services, and transportation details described in this story are all historically accurate. Some of my favorite details include the separate unaccompanied woman's entrance, the golden cage elevator, electric lighting powered by the hotel's own powerhouse, bathhouse barrel horses, the ostridge farm, the annunciator (button for calling staff to a guest room), the billiard room, the Crown Room, the hotel library, rotunda, and the railcars. Even the peculiar shape of the hallway near Lottie's room (which allowed Eleanore to eavesdrop) was based on a historical blueprint showing the floor and room in which she stayed.

Two fun facts I wasn't able to work into the story are that the powerhouse had its own automatic sprinkler system and a tunnel that connected the powerhouse to the hotel, both of which I learned about while taking a history tour at the hotel. I highly recommend taking this tour if you're ever in the area.

For those of you who've read my Chaparral Hearts series, you might have recognized that I gave a cameo to one of those characters in this book. If you did, please let me know! If you missed it, you can flip back to the scene where Thomas is escorting Eleanore and Aunt Gladys to San Diego with the intent of finding a private investigator. His plans are waylaid by an overly helpful citizen named Margaret Thompson. Margaret was the heroine of my novel, *Harmony on the Horizon,* and would have been sixty-four years old at the time she encounters Aunt Gladys on the ferry.

GET ALL THE BOOKS IN THE ROMANCE AT THE GILDED AGE RESORTS SERIES

Book 1: A Winter at the White Queen

Book 2: A Summer at Sagamore

Book 3: A Season at the Grand

Book 4: A Summer at Thousand Island House

Book 5: Christmas at the Jekyll Island Club

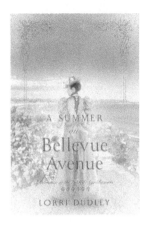

Book 6: A Summer on Bellevue Avenue

Book 7: A Spring at the Greenbrier

Book 8: A Summer at The Niagara of the South

Book 9: A Christmas at Hotel del Coronado

Did you enjoy this book? We hope so!
**Would you take a quick minute to leave a review
where you purchased the book?**
It doesn't have to be long. Just a sentence or two telling
what you liked about the story!

Receive a FREE ebook and get updates when new Wild
Heart books release: https://wildheartbooks.org/
newsletter

ABOUT THE AUTHOR

Kathleen Denly lives in sunny California with her loving husband, four children, two dogs, and ten cats. As a member of the adoption and foster community, children in need are a cause dear to her heart and she finds they make frequent appearances in her stories. When she isn't writing, researching, or caring for children, Kathleen spends her time reading, visiting historical sites, hiking, and crafting.

If you love historical romance, check out the other Wild Heart books!

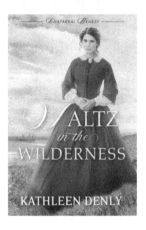

Waltz in the Wilderness by Kathleen Denly

She's desperate to find her missing father. His conscience demands he risk all to help.

Eliza Brooks is haunted by her role in her mother's death, so she'll do anything to find her missing pa— even if it means sneaking aboard a southbound ship. When those meant to protect her abandon and betray her instead, a family friend's unexpected assistance is a blessing she can't refuse.

Daniel Clarke came to California to make his fortune, and a stable job as a San Francisco carpenter has earned him more than most have scraped from the local goldfields. But it's been four years since he left Massachusetts and his fiancé is impatient for his return. Bound for home at last, Daniel Clarke finds his heart and plans challenged by a tenacious young woman with haunted eyes. Though every word he utters seems to offend her, he is determined to see her safely returned to her father. Even if that means risking his fragile engagement.

When disaster befalls them in the remote wilderness of the Southern California mountains, true feelings are revealed, and both must face heart-rending decisions. But how to decide when every choice before them leads to someone getting hurt?

∾

An Uncertain Road by Abbey Downey

A female auto racer, a mechanic determined to walk away from the sport, and the race of a lifetime...

When young widow Flora Montfort returns to America, she's determined to use her training in auto racing to support herself and her French mother-in-law—even if female drivers are rare in 1905. So when the owner of a successful sporting goods store hires her to drive in the Glidden Tour, a ten-day race through New England, she jumps at the opportunity.

Jensen Gable must be convinced that joining the team as the ride-along mechanic is worth the risk. After losing his best friend in a tragic racing accident, Jensen has vowed never to participate in the sport again. But his promise to protect that friend's younger brother, also on the tour, is the only thing that outweighs his fear of the dangers.

As they race through New England, Flora and Jensen find common ground that ignites their interest in each other, but doubts and old enemies come between them. Hazardous road conditions, meddling locals, and competitors who'll stop at nothing to win—they all conspire to prevent Flora and Jensen from reaching the finish line. As the race of a lifetime heats up, one question rises above all others...can their love find the road that leads to forever?

∾

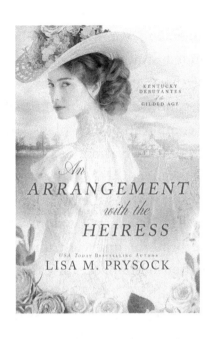

An Arrangement by the Heiress by Lisa M. Prysock

She's a wealthy debutante with the finest ancestry in Kentucky horseracing circles...

He's a member of New York's Gilded Age elite, yet on the brink of financial ruin...

Neither of them want an arranged marriage...or do they?

Veronica Lyndon has a plan for her life, and it doesn't include being married off to a perfect stranger. After all, she is descended from generations of Kentucky horseracing royalty. She has no need for a marriage arranged solely to secure her place among the elite of Manhattan's Gilded Age society. But that's exactly what her parents expect of her. Determined to defy the arrangement, Veronica formulates a plan to drive her intended away. But when Edward arrives in anticipation of the match, she doesn't expect to find him so attractive, nor can she deny the feelings he stirs in her heart, complicating her plans. Has true love galloped into her life by conventional means, or are her estimations mistaken?

Edward Beckett realizes the futility of avoiding the arranged marriage to Miss Lyndon. His family is already on the brink of financial ruin and Veronica's dowry may be their best opportunity to recover. But he didn't expect to fall for the Kentucky debutante so easily. He finds himself attracted to her natural beauty and vivacious spirit, free from the conventions of other ladies in his customary circles. In fact, he's downright smitten after meeting Veronica. Unfortunately, Edward's sisters don't feel the same, and if their attempts to sabotage the relationship are successful, his whirlwind courtship to Veronica may be over before it's really begun.

Saddle up for a clean romp filled with sweet romance, inspiration, and plenty of adventure along this course of obstacles and a glide through the splendor and opulence of the Gilded Age.